THE NIGHT

MAY ARCHER

Cover by Cate Ashwood
Professional Beta Read by Leslie Copeland
Proofed by Susie Selva

Acknowledgments

As always, thank you to Leslie Copeland for being an amazing overlord/beta reader/friend!! Your notes give me life!

Thank you to Susie Selva, who quotes from style manuals and also somehow remembers that Joe Cross doesn't *actually* live in O'Leary. *Overflow brain 4eva.*

Thanks to Cate Ashwood for an amazing cover (and endless patience).

The biggest, hugest, most *splendiferous* thanks to the posse for helping me get this book written in record time and for brightening my life in ways large and small. I am a seriously lucky individual to count you people as my friends. Special thanks to:

Macy Blake, my golden girl, for helping me plot a quick little novella (one of these days I will write short, but today was not that day) and for being all *"lean in to the Hallmark!"*

Neve, for alpha reading, and sanity checking, and cheerleading, and saying "but maybe a blowjob..."

Lucy, for the early morning/late night sprints, and for *getting it.*

Hailey, for sending cats right when I need them, and for the transcontinental Jack Ryan bae-watch.

And, as always, thank you to all of you lovely people for reading and loving these guys!! O'Leary wouldn't exist without you. <3

For my husband: Thank you for 20 improbably, imperfectly magical years of marriage. And thanks for making me watch Hallmark Christmas movies every single day in July (...and October... and November... and December).

And for the Archer spawn: Thanks for your unending random trivia, your unmitigated sass, and your genuine kindness. I love you guys beyond... but you know that.

One night in Vegas, I gave him my heart... one day later, he broke it.

Look, I've never claimed to be a nice guy. I don't do pretty words, I don't give polite smiles, and I refuse to be sucked into the sappy bucket of sentimentality that is Christmas in small town O'Leary, New York at Christmastime. Smiling neighbors, overly decorated trees, a town parade, a *Santa contest?* Ho ho *no*. I do shifts as a firefighter, and I go home alone.

I fell into the trap once—that stupid night in Vegas— of believing there was more out there for me. I took a chance on a guy with magical green eyes and a gorgeous smile. The next day, Liam McKnight was gone. He took my heart with him... and left his wedding ring behind.

Except now my once-upon-a-time husband is in O'Leary with a *kid* in tow, there are carols, lights, and cookies everywhere I turn, and worst of all? The spark between us burns brighter than ever, because whatever happened in Vegas definitely didn't stay there. Liam came to town looking for an ending, but what's building between us feels an awful lot like a beginning. Too bad it's going to take more than a dozen interfering O'Learians to convince me to take a second chance on heartache, on love... on us.

Chapter One

LIAM

FUNNY HOW FIVE YEARS COULD CHANGE THINGS.

Back then, I'd loved to travel. I'd traveled for jobs, I'd traveled for fun, and really, it had all been one and the same for a professional photographer who was thrilled on the daily by his work.

I vaguely remembered a life where I kept a carry-on in the closet, pre-packed with my passport, camera, and maybe five or six other minimalist travel essentials, trusting I could acquire anything else I needed when I got where I was going.

My editor needed me in Budapest? My sister wanted to spend Christmas in Seychelles? Some hot guy invited me to Steamboat in January? *Yes, yes, yes.*

Nowadays, a seven-hour car trip required four days of planning, three whole suitcases, and an internet deep-dive into reviews of the rest areas along I-90—*yes, those were an actual thing*—so I could map out our stops with a kind of devotedness I'd once only applied to my craft.

And still? Despite all my best efforts?

"But you *said* you would *pack them*!" My daughter's big

1

brown eyes met mine in the Volvo's rearview mirror, wide with the kind of accusation and outrage that only a forgotten bag of red-frosted Santa cookies from the Stop & Shop could engender. "You *said!*"

"I know." I ran a hand through my hair and reminded myself to be patient. "In my defense, I did remember to pack my suitcase, your clothes suitcase, an entire second suitcase full of toys you can play with when we get to the hotel in Syracuse tonight, your stationery and markers so you can write more letters to Santa Claus, and a whole cooler full of healthy snacks." Along with the folder full of papers my attorney had drawn up, tucked into a brown leather messenger bag and riding shotgun. "*And*, the cookies will still be there when we get home tomorrow night—"

"But I asked you *three times*, Daddy! And you said, 'Hazel Grace McKnight, for the love of all that's holy in the universe, stop asking me about the cookies!' So I *did*. And you *forgot them anyway*."

"Yes. I know. Thanks for the recap." Just in case I'd forgotten. Or begun to think positively about my parenting skills. "Bug, I will buy you a cookie as soon as we see a place that sells cookies. Promise." I peered out the window at the desolate road surrounded by forest and wondered if we'd be in Canada before that happened.

"Fine. But you'll need to buy me *several* cookies. " She blinked guilelessly, a sure sign I was being conned. "Because I had *several* cookies at home, and fair is fair."

I snorted. Who taught kids this crazy stuff?

Oh, right. Me.

"How much longer?" she asked.

"GPS says twenty minutes to O'Leary." I spoke like this was an actual fact, though I saw almost no signs of civilization except for a couple of unmarked driveways and a speed limit sign with a Christmas wreath hanging beneath it. "Hang tight, kiddo."

The road was strangely appealing—curving and nearly hidden in some places, straight and flat and arched with trees in others—and the whole idea of some paths being obscured while others were straightforward was so perfectly metaphorical that part of me itched to pull over and grab my camera so I could document the play of light and shadow. In the time I referred to as BH—Before Hazel—I wouldn't have hesitated, even if the road was narrow and a little dangerous. Before Hazel, my *camera* would have been riding shotgun.

Now, my Canon was buried in the trunk under fifty pounds of Hazel-related clothing and accessories, and the tiny dictator in the backseat would have me flogged if I made her spend even a minute longer in the car than absolutely necessary.

The weirdest part was, I really didn't mind the change at all most of the time.

"You could turn up the music," Hazel suggested.

Okay, I didn't *altogether* mind the change.

The music Hazel was referring to—a little album called *Kiddie Bop Christmas.* Perhaps you've heard of it?— was a form of torture surely outlawed by the Geneva Convention, and yet somehow still widely available in stores, where just anyone's crazy sister could find it, buy it, and send it to her seven-year-old niece *eight entire weeks before Christmas.* After seven hours in the car, my eyelid had begun twitching to the rhythm of "Jingle Bell Rock."

And, just to say, I really hoped my sister was enjoying her month-long motorcycle trek across Mongolia because payback would be swift and painful once *Auntie Livvy* was stateside again.

"How about we talk instead," I suggested.

"Talk?" she said in a tone that probably perfectly fore-shadowed her teenage years.

"Yes, *talk*. That thing with the voices where we say what we're thinking."

Hazel giggled, then immediately sobered, clasped her hands under her chin, and stared sadly out the window, the very picture of a Dickensian street urchin. "I'm thinking, '*Oh, good heavens, I do so love cookies*,'" she said in a flawless British accent.

I pressed my lips together to keep from smiling. *Well-played, kid. Though possibly over-acted.*

"Wow. Those hours watching *Peppa Pig* have really paid off, haven't they?"

"Maybe." Her eyes met mine in the mirror. "Mrs. Boudreaux only lets us watch kid shows at her house."

Mrs. Boudreaux, our seventy-year-old neighbor, was the epitome of a kindly grandmother—short and stout, with curly white hair and reading glasses she could never seem to find, though she wore them on a beaded string around her neck. She definitely erred on the side of caution when it came to *anything* on television—a fact I appreciated, and Hazel did not.

"Mrs. Boudreaux is a very kind and responsible person, which is why I trust her to take care of you when I have meetings or need to work late," I informed her. "You can wait to watch *Wild Nature* and your Michio Kaku documen-taries when I'm home."

"But nature is *fascinating*."

"I know."

"And learning about black holes is educational."

"Uh huh."

She was quiet for a second, then said, "I just really hate it when you work late. I might *possibly* get *slightly* scared when you're gone. And everything's better when you're there."

My stomach clenched with the guilt and worry that had basically been my constant companions since Hazel was a toddler. *Was I gone too much? Was I taking care of her appropriately? Was I raising her the way Nora would want? Was I enough?*

"I hate it too, sweets." Then, because you were supposed to be honest with your kids or something, I clarified, "I mean, I like photography, but I miss you a lot."

"You could just take pictures during the day. Mrs. Boudreaux says nothing good happens after dark anyway."

I gritted my teeth and slightly revised my opinion of Mrs. Boudreaux. "That's one way of looking at things," I said, hopefully diplomatically. "But I don't only take pictures of daytime stuff. When my boss wants pictures of a specific event that's at night, I have to go."

Hazel nodded, pondered this silently for a minute, then grinned. "It'll be fine, Daddy. I'm gonna ask Santa to fix it for Christmas. I'm asking for a cat, a big house, a baby sister or brother, a real Christmas tree, and to become a princess."

"Are you?" Figured it wouldn't be anything, you know, *attainable*. I pressed my lips together again, this time for a different reason. "Hazel…" I began, then faltered.

Dear Gossip Girl: How old was too old for your daughter to believe in Santa Claus? At what age did the letters written in tipsy capitals and the ceremonial walk to drop the envelope in the mailbox become *lying*? At what age did you have to kill her innocence if you ever wanted your daughter to trust you as an adult?

These were some of the many, many parenting questions I had, and it was times like this when I wished I had a partner, or a local parent group, or hell, parents in this time zone to consult. Turned out, when you suddenly inherited your best friend's toddler kidlet, she didn't come with an instruction manual. See also: no safety net. For either of us. I was learning shit as I went along, in real time, and sometimes I was absolutely certain I was fucking it all up.

Laughing brown eyes—eyes *so exactly* like Nora's that I sometimes did a double-take—watched me in the mirror, and Hazel's dark curls bounced against her red jacket as she shook her head. "You're wondering when to tell me Santa's fake, aren't you?"

I don't know why the things that came out of her mouth still surprised me sometimes. Hazel was seven going on thirty-five, which made her just slightly older than me, and she called me on my shit—another trait she shared with her mother—with remarkable frequency. Sometimes, looking at Hazel, I missed Nora so badly I could cry, even five years after the car accident that had left Hazel an orphan.

It was a little bit of a reprieve when the GPS interrupted to inform us it was time to turn off the twisty road and onto a residential street with a hopeful little sign that read "Welcome to O'Leary, Population: 1074."

"See, the thing is, Bug…" I cleared my throat, opened my mouth to say… I didn't even know what… when Hazel interrupted.

"It's cool, Daddy. Don't stress. I already decided Santa's real."

I shut my mouth with a clack. "You decided it."

"Sure," said my pint-sized philosopher with another of her shrugs. "He's real because I believe he's real."

And… *damn*. That was some next-level ish right there. The kind of shit that made you wonder if maybe you were born knowing things that life made you forget.

"Well." I cleared my throat again. "Just in case, I think I won't quit my day job yet. But hopefully things will change in the future. Maybe…" I hesitated. "Maybe you won't have to stay with Mrs. Boudreaux when I'm gone for much longer."

I'd been saving *fanatically* to fund a sabbatical from my usual contract jobs and work on my photography book full time. It was a crazy dream, and I knew it. Everyone I'd confided in about it said so. And I was pretty sure I wouldn't be able to make it happen *immediately*. But some-day, maybe I'd be able to work fewer hours and spend more time with Hazel. Maybe I'd be able to do work I actually enjoyed and found fulfilling again. Maybe I'd be able to resuscitate my practically non-existent love life too.

Just as soon as I took care of one teeny, tiny little piece of unfin-ished business in O'Leary, I thought, with another glance at the bag on the passenger's seat.

"This isn't about Scott, is it?" Hazel asked, suspicious as a cat.

"What? No." My smile faded. "But what's wrong with Scott? He's a friend of mine. And he likes you very much."

She shook her head sadly at my naïveté. "He likes *you* very much."

I released a loud breath. Hazel wasn't wrong. Scott— the tall, dark, handsome, successful journalist with the toned body and the hair that fell *just so* over one eye—had started out as a colleague I'd met while covering local poli-tics and had quickly become a friend, sort of. But it was fairly obvious—apparently even to seven-year-olds—he wanted more, and I was fairly sure I was going to give it to him…

Again, once I'd tied up this one teeny, tiny—*did I mention how teeny-tiny it was?*—loose end.

"Hey, now! Didn't Scott talk with you about the

pictures you were coloring when we were at the coffee shop last weekend? He's making an effort to get to know you."

She pursed her lips. "He suggested I color inside the lines."

"Oh."

"Like a big girl."

I winced. "Okay, okay. Look, I said he was *trying*, not that he was succeeding. *Yet*. Some guys don't have a lot of experience with kids your age, babe. Give him time—"

"He called me Bug."

"*I* call you Bug!"

"Because you're *my father*. No one else can call me that unless I say. And he got very *huffy* when I told him so."

I ran my tongue over my teeth. On the one hand, I was glad my lessons on personal boundaries had taken root. On the other…

"Also? Scott won't drink hot cocoa because he doesn't put processed foods or refined sugar in his body, he thinks Beyoncé's talent is overhyped, and he has a *pet bird*."

I blinked. I… didn't know any of those things about Scott. But then, I'd never bothered to ask, and I didn't doubt Hazel *had*.

Sometimes my overwhelming *like* of her swamped me. I mean, I'd *loved* her from the first moment I saw her, all red-faced and scrappy, snuggled in Jake and Nora's arms, but you couldn't help loving people sometimes. It wasn't always voluntary. *Liking* someone was an entirely different matter.

"What's wrong with having a pet bird?" I demanded. "You've been harassing me for a pet for months!"

"I don't trust anything that doesn't have whites in its eyes," she said, like this should be obvious, and I wondered if maybe I should quit photography altogether and spend my time writing a book called *Life Advice from Hazel*. I wasn't sure if it would be shelved under comedy or self-help, but either way, it was bound to be a bestseller. "And besides, I have been asking you for a *cat*. Cats and birds are *mortal enemies*."

"Bug," I said patiently. "Scott's a nice guy. He's got a good job. And he's hard-working and responsible."

"Hmm." She narrowed her eyes. "Well, if nice and responsible's what you're looking for, Mrs. Boudreaux is single."

I gaped. *Direct fucking hit.* "Listen to the sass! Who even *are* you right now?" I demanded.

She sat back in her booster seat with a self-satisfied smile. "Your daughter."

Yes. Yes, she definitely was. And she was worth any sacrifice of time or money or effort or—I swallowed and glanced at the passenger's seat, a bit guiltily this time—or *anything*.

"You can just chill right the heck out, *daughter*, because I'm not marrying Scott or *anyone*," I informed her.

"Ever?" She frowned.

"Ever."

More specifically, I wasn't marrying anyone ever *again*. I was busy trying to dissolve a relationship, not get into one.

Hazel sighed and kicked at the back of my seat. "How much longer *now*?"

"Uh, less than two minutes. We're basically there," I said.

"Where's *there*?"

"I told you. A tiny town called O'Leary."

"And why are we here?"

I hesitated. "I have some forms I need to get signed for my attorney."

She frowned. "What kind of forms?"

"Hmmm, how about *the kind that are grown-up business*?" I was starting to feel a bit queasy as we got closer to O'Leary… which was stupid, really. This was gonna be easy-peasy.

A two-minute job. A scribble on a piece of paper to cancel out another scribble on another piece of paper.

A task I should have completed years ago, and one that would never have had to be done in the first place, if I hadn't been an absolute *sucker* for a sexy smile, a deep voice, laughing golden-brown eyes, and an instant spark of connection that couldn't possibly have been *half* as soul-meltingly meaningful as I'd thought at the time.

A chore I wouldn't have to do *now*, if the things that happened one night in Vegas ever *really* stayed in Vegas.

Who could a guy sue for false advertising? Asking for a friend.

I cleared my throat. "Besides, I thought it would be fun to take a road trip together. Are you saying you wish I'd left you with Mrs. Boudreaux *overnight*?"

"Maybe! Now that I know she's your *perfect girlfriend*, maybe I could have made her fall in *looooove* with you!"

"Wow, yes, and then she could move in with us forever, and I would totally put her in charge of screen time. Isn't she allergic to cats, Bug? You're so selfless to give all that up for the sake of my true love!"

Hazel mock pouted. "You're mean."

"I know," I sang.

"Can we put up our Christmas tree this weekend? Can it be a *real* tree this year?"

I sighed. The small, fake tree in our storage unit got sadder and more dilapidated every year, but also…

"How many times have I explained that our landlord doesn't allow real trees, Bug? But yes, we can put up our tree."

"And buy a new ornament for this year too?"

"Sure."

"And I can pick it out?"

"Absolutely, you can."

I slowed down to take a gander at the sleepy little town. O'Leary's center appeared to be one wide street lined with slanted parking spaces. On both sides, brick and white clapboard storefronts were already decked out for the holidays, and adults and children alike stood chatting in merry little groups before them.

"This town looks... odd," I said aloud, looking at a lit-up train display in the window of a hardware store. It was like the town had transported itself in time from 1950-something, and only the cars and the people were new. *Oh.* And the rainbow pride flag hanging out in front of one of the stores. That too.

"This town looks *fun*," Hazel corrected, leaning forward to get a better look out the window. "Like a carnival. Look at all the Christmas decorations! And look at that girl's coat! I would *treasure* a coat with purple sparkles beyond *anything* in the entire *world*. And—" Hazel let out a blood-curdling scream. "*Oh my God, Daddy! Stop the car! Stop the car right now!*"

I pressed my foot all the way down on the brake, coming to a screeching halt in the center of the street that had the Volvo rocking back on its rear wheels. "What?" I demanded, shifting into Park and unbuckling my belt. "Are you okay, baby? Did you hurt yourself? Did you—"

"*There's a bakery right there!*" Hazel bounced up and down in her seat, curls shimmying as she pointed excitedly out the window. "Bakeries sell *cookies*!"

"Are you... *Christ alive*, are you *kidding* me? For heaven's sake, I thought you were dying, Hazel!" I clapped a hand to my heart, which was about to beat out of my chest, and scowled at the face in the mirror.

"But I *am*," she said solemnly. "I am *dying* for *cookies*! Please can we go? Please?"

I checked the GPS again. The address I'd found on Google earlier this week was about a half mile down the road, and it was already mid-afternoon. If I wanted to get back to Syracuse by bedtime, I had to finish my business here by six at the latest. And if he wasn't home, or if the address was wrong and I had to ask around, it could take a while to—

"You *promised*, Daddy."

"Oh, fine." I swung into a parking spot outside a quaint-looking little bakery called *Fanaille*. "*One* cookie. And no more screaming, Hazel Grace. Got it?"

"Got it," Hazel promised, staring out the windshield at the bakery with shining eyes, like she had seen the Promised Land and found it was made of sugar.

"These better be the best darn cookies in the universe," I grumbled. I pushed open my door.

"They will," she assured me confidently, unbuckling her belt and jumping out of the car. "They'll be the best, most magical cookies ever." She grabbed my hand and towed me toward the door. "And all that magic is just sitting there waiting for us."

Chapter Two

GIDEON

Once upon a time, I'd announced over Thanksgiving dinner that I was taking a job heading up the fire department in tiny O'Leary, New York, and my entire family had stared at me like I'd lost my mind.

"But it'll be so quiet," my sister had said, wrinkling her nose. "How will you stand it?"

"You'll be all alone," my mother had said worriedly, and my father had finished her thought, as usual, adding, "And in those small towns, you're a pariah if they find out you're gay."

Little did they fucking know.

"Gideon! Hey, Gideon, wait!" Joe Cross jogged across the street and stepped in front of me as I walked down Weaver Street with my hands jammed in the pockets of my leather jacket. "Didn't you hear me calling you, buddy? You must be half-asleep. Here, take a flyer!"

I stopped and glanced down at the stack of red and green papers he held, then back up at Joe. He was decked in head-to-toe *Santa*—which, considering the man's white beard, pink cheeks, and beer gut was less like him wearing a costume and more like him becoming the most fully actualized version of himself—and he was smiling in a way that dared you not to smile back.

Challenge accepted.

I stared at him impassively and said, "No."

"N-no?" He blinked. "But I didn't ask you to do anything except take a—"

"Flyer," I finished. "I know. Angela Ross already attempted to hand me one at the fire station. Con tried to give me one on the street corner. I'm fully expecting Micah to pop out of the fucking doorway of Blooms"—I nodded toward Micah's flower shop—"and accost me again. I'm not biting. Count me out."

"But…" Joe looked down at the flyers in confusion. "I ain't inviting you to church for religious conversion night, Gideon. It's only a Santa contest, man. Gonna be held before the Light Parade a week from Saturday, and participants get twenty percent off a Christmas tree at the Ross Landscaping tree lot over by the playground. We'll even provide the costumes! It's all in good fun."

"Fun." I pursed my lips like I was tasting the word. "Joe, do you know how I spent my evening?"

He licked his lips. "Uh. No?"

"Working a double shift, fighting fires. That's *fires*, Joe. As in, the fucking *plural* of fire."

"Oh." His face cleared. "Man. You must be beat."

"I am," I agreed. "I'm very definitely beat. And this morning, I need coffee more than I need oxygen. Coffee that's *right there*." I clasped his shoulder with one hand, turned him, and held my other hand out toward *Fanaille*, shining like a caffeine-and-sugar-laden beacon in the distance. "So close I can almost taste it."

"Morning? *Heh*. S'more like afternoon, Gideon. It's after two—" I squeezed Joe's shoulder firmly and he cleared his throat. "Though, I ah… I guess it must seem like morning, if you've been working all night?"

"You'd guess right," I approved. "And Joe? Right now, you're standing between me and the thing I need to survive. Does that sound… *wise*?"

"Uh. No?"

"No," I confirmed sadly. "But worse than that? Worse than *that*? You're trying to hand out papers that are gonna end up strewn all over the street in a few hours. You're simultaneously creating litter *and* wasting precious natural resources. Are you singlehandedly trying to destroy the earth, Joe?"

"What? No! Course not! But it's… it's for *Christmas*."

I snorted. "*It's for Christmas*. Here's a fact for you to ponder. This town can go *weeks* without a fucking fire. Weeks without even a malfunctioning smoke detector! And then suddenly? Thanksgiving rolls around, and my tiny, black heart starts to beat double-time with pure fear. Do you know why that is, Joe?"

"Uh. No?"

"Because it means Christmas is coming. *Christmas*, as in the time of year when people purposely bring highly flammable *decaying shrubbery* inside their homes, festoon it with *electrical wires*, place brightly wrapped *kindling* underneath it, and say '*It's so fucking magical*.' You know what's not magical, Joe?"

"Uh." His voice went up an octave and his eyes widened. "No?"

"Spending the evening standing outside in the cold pouring water on a blaze, while the wind whips the fucking spray into your hair and freezes your ears into icicles. Definitely does *not* fill a man with holiday spirit. You get me?"

"But," Joe ventured gamely. "But you wanna support

your community, right? Peace on earth, good will toward men?"

I stared at him for a long moment, letting him fidget, then I leaned in close like I was imparting a secret. "I think if a man truly wanted a peaceful planet, he'd leave the trees in the forest, and if he was *really* about goodwill, he'd let his neighbor get some coffee."

Joe frowned down at his papers again like they'd betrayed him somehow.

I clapped his shoulder once. "Alrighty, then. You have a nice day!" I didn't wait for his response before moving on down the street.

A pariah? Yeah, not so much.

Less than twenty feet later, another voice called out.

"Hey, yo, Gideon!"

Why was the world hell-bent on keeping me from coffee?

But though I didn't stop or turn around—and I would never admit it even under torture—*this* voice made me slow down just slightly. Just enough for Parker Hoffstraeder to catch up to me.

I couldn't say why I had a soft spot for Parker in particular, of all the folks in O'Leary. Maybe because he persevered even when life dealt him a shitty hand, or maybe because he was snarky and funny, or maybe because he had these big, perpetually excited green eyes that reminded me of…

Nope. I smothered that thought like a hot spot. *Parker reminded me of no one.*

And shit, I must *really* be tired if I was having to force myself not to think about the person Parker definitely didn't remind me of.

Parker came up alongside me, and I glanced at him from the corner of my eye. Sweet Jesus. *He* was in Santa gear too, though at least he'd limited himself to just the hat and the giant black sack he carried over his shoulder. Still, this level of Christmas fervor was insane, even for O'Leary.

"Howdy, Parker. Quite a fashion-forward look you're sporting."

"What'd you do to Joe Cross?" he demanded, falling into step with me as we strode up Weaver. He hooked a thumb over his shoulder. "Man looks like his dog died! I thought something had happened to Tom Brady."

I snorted. Joe was possibly the biggest Patriots fan in the world—certainly in the greater O'Leary area. It was probably a good thing I hadn't remembered that while talking to him.

"I didn't do anything to him."

"Uh huh."

"I didn't!" I made a crossing motion over my heart.

"Why don't I believe you?"

"Because you're a really suspicious soul, and you should probably work on that?"

Parker side-eyed me and I felt my lips twitch. He was adorable, really, and if we'd met a few years ago—and he hadn't been disgustingly in love with Jamie Burke even then—there might have been a spark of something there, but as it was, my feelings toward him weren't remotely sexual. Which was handy, really, since Jamie was built as solidly as I was, and happened to be possessive as hell.

"I might possibly have implied that Joe was selfishly destroying the planet by handing out flyers in his quest for holiday ho-ho-hos," I admitted. "But it's no less than the truth."

"*Jesus.*" Parker threw his head back and looked to the sky for divine intervention. "Congratulations. You are officially the grumpiest, Scroogiest, Grinchiest person in town."

I rolled my eyes. I so was *not*.

Parker sighed and shifted the sack off his back so he was holding it on his hip like a baby. He wasn't a particularly big guy, and the thing looked heavy, and though I knew before I even opened my mouth that I was gonna regret asking, I couldn't help it. "You need a hand?"

"Nah. It's awkward, not heavy. It's a bunch of Santa costumes. I'm handing them out to everyone who signed up for the contest because we're all gonna start wearing them next week." He grinned. "I have a couple extras. Want one?"

"Christ, no. You know, the Grinch gets a bad rap, but when you think about it, the dude just wanted to be left alone. You know what's *really* awful? A red-suited, beady-eyed creeper who spies on people all the damn time. He sees me when I'm sleeping? He knows when I'm awake? Like, what the *fuck* is that even *about*, Parker?"

He sighed gustily but didn't look surprised. "It's like you're allergic to fun, Gideon."

"Or like I'm baffled by people's misplaced sentimentality for a random, overly commercial holiday, but sure. Let's go with your version."

Parker's smile turned crafty. "Which brings me to my other reason for catching up to you today."

I stopped in the middle of the sidewalk next to Spinning Jenny's laundromat. "I swear to God, Parker, if you try to hand me a flyer…"

Parker laughed. "I wouldn't. I *couldn't*! Do you see a flyer in my hand?"

I glared at the sack with narrowed eyes, and Parker laughed again. "No flyers in there either," he promised.

I folded my arms over my chest. "So what *do* you want?"

"Simple." His grin widened. "I want to unveil my plan to make you a happier person."

"Your… *what?*"

"See…" Parker set the sack on the ground and his hands on his hips. "If you'd bothered to read one of the flyers, you'd know that the whole *point* of the Santa contest is to do good deeds for your neighbors—"

"Oh, good God! Did someone actually think it was a good idea to give the people of this town *additional reason* not to mind their own business?"

"It's about O'Learians helping O'Learians, Gideon! Peace on earth, goodwill toward—"

"I'm moving," I declared, holding up a hand. "Leaving town. Effective immediately. I will not take part in this, neither as a…a *Santa* nor as a victim of your Santa shenanigans."

"Move? And leave that sweet little colonial up on Markham that you fixed up *all by yourself?* No, you won't, and everyone knows it." Parker gave me a beatific smile and his eyes shone. "So, let's cut to the chase! Gideon Mason, *you* need a date. And it's gonna be my special Christmas project to find you one."

"*Fuck me,*" I moaned.

"Exactly," he said, wiggling his eyebrows underneath his stupid Santa hat.

"This is not happening, Parker." I resumed walking toward the bakery, because while I suspected there was not enough coffee in the universe to conquer this day, there was a base minimum amount required to endure it. "I'd thank you for thinking of me, if you weren't being such an interfering, presumptuous brat, but you are. So."

"I was thinking maybe *Brian.*" Parker lurched along after me, still toting the stupid sack.

"I'm not listening."

"I mean, Brian is Jamie's ex, which makes the situation —" Parker cleared his throat. "You know."

"Really fucking weird, since you're Jamie's current arm candy?"

"*Complicated*," Parker corrected defiantly. "Since Jamie and I are *in love and in a committed relationship*."

"Potato, po-tah-to."

"But Brian and I are kinda friends now," Parker went on. "Or *friendly*, anyway, so…"

I stopped walking again.

"How does *that* work?" I wanted to know. "Do you discuss Jamie's sex noises? Critique his performance and endurance? Commiserate about all his terrible habits and the weird lump in the shape of California on his ass?"

Parker's cheeks went a very un-Santa Claus shade of red. "*No!* We very carefully *do not* discuss anything of the kind! And for your information, Jamie's ass is *flawless*." His eyes flashed. "But if you think I'm going to drop my idea because you're being a bastard, you're wrong. You're only making me more committed. So…*back to Brian.*"

"Back to not listening." I walked on.

"Brian's a little bit… bruised, I guess," Parker said, hurrying after me. "He's a great guy. Super sweet. But I think he needs someone a little older, a little more settled. You know, kind of a Daddy."

A Daddy? I stopped with my hand on the bakery door and glared at him. "And you immediately thought of *me*?"

"Well, I…" He swallowed. "Kinda?"

"I… truly have no words right now, Parks. But stick around and I'll think of a couple."

I yanked open the door and stepped inside *Fanaille*, where the air reeked of butter, cinnamon, and blessed, blessed coffee. It made my mouth water, which was the only reason I didn't turn around, walk right back out, and drive my ass home. Instead, I took a spot at the end of a five-person line, stared at my boots, and tried to ignore the Santa reject who'd followed me inside.

"I didn't mean it like *that*," he insisted, standing in line behind me.

I turned my head to glare. "I don't care *what* way you meant it," I said in a fierce whisper, "but I can goddamn fucking guarantee you, I'm nobody's *Daddy*. Not literally, and sure as *fuck* not figuratively. I'm only thirty-nine years old!"

"Okay. *Okay*!" Parker's face flamed. "But you know, it's more of a vibe, not an age thing! You're a solid, dependable guy. And you've got that whole silver fox aesthetic, with the hair." With his free hand, he gestured toward my head, and I couldn't help scrubbing my fingers over the short strands, like I could erase whatever it was about them that screamed *Daddy*.

Parker cleared his throat and scratched at the back of his neck. "So, ah, not Brian then?"

I stared at him wordlessly.

"Right. Yes," he said hurriedly. "Definitely not Brian. Okay, then. Do you know Reggie Carbury?"

"Parker." I took a deep breath. "I'm not sure how to say this so you'll understand, since English doesn't seem to be working. This is not happening. I don't date. I *do not* date. It's not for a lack of available men, okay? It's not because I lack confidence or opportunity. It's because *I don't want to.* So please go find yourself an orphan who needs a family for Christmas, or a homeless kitty who needs a friend for Hanukkah, because I'm not playing along."

"Isn't rescuing kittens kind of *your* thing?" Parker grinned mischievously, completely undeterred, and I gnashed my teeth.

"I can't believe you brought that up. That was *one*

time!" I hissed. "Months ago. And I had no idea anyone was taking my damn picture, let alone that the fucking thing was gonna be all over the internet."

"But you looked so hot, all decked out in your fire gear, with the little orange puff ball cuddled against your big, manly chest! Ovaries and movaries exploded all over New York." Parker fluttered his eyelashes.

Once again, I was confident I would regret asking, but… "Movaries?"

"Oh, that's ah, male ovaries?" Parker twisted his mouth to one side. "Pretty sure it's a thing. Or possibly I made it up."

"Jesus." I scrubbed at my hair again. "*Why* would you make that up?"

"Well, you know when you see an adorable baby and you get the sudden, temporary urge to have a kid just so you can squish its cheeks all day?"

"No."

"Okay, well have you ever seen a hot guy doing something super sweet, like perhaps *cuddling* said cute baby or, say, nestling a tiny kitten against his chest, and you kinda feel simultaneously protective and aroused?"

"No."

Parker sighed. "Well then possibly you were born without movaries."

"I think that's *very* likely. *Since they don't exist.*" I lifted my eyes to the ceiling and shook my head.

This would be the day I was finally driven to insanity by the populace of O'Leary. And I *still* didn't have a damn coffee in my hand.

Ash Martin, one of the co-owners of the bakery, glanced in our direction and lifted his chin when he saw Parker. It wasn't often that I looked at Ash and saw the Navy SEAL he used to be—frankly, it was hard to remember he hadn't always been behind the counter at *Fanaille* with Cal, or that he and Cal hadn't always been a thing—but sometimes it came through in his eyes or in the way he moved his bulky frame like he wasn't six and a half feet tall and shaped like an inverted triangle.

Ash finished making a coffee and handed it over with a smile, then stepped up close behind Cal, bracing his hands on Cal's hips. He leaned down and whispered something in Cal's ear that made Cal turn his red head in our direction, then look all the way up at Ash. He whispered something back, leaning his head against Ash's chest, and his lips quirked at the corners like he was giving Ash shit, but his eyes were too caramel-soft to really pull off the snarkiness that used to be his trademark. Caelan James, who was once the crankiest person in O'Leary, was head over heels for his fiancé and didn't care who knew it.

And according to Parker, now I'd inherited his title.

I frowned down at the black and white floor tiles.

It wasn't like I was grumpy on purpose. People just pissed me off. And it wasn't that I reacted negatively to *everything* in the world, just to stupid, trivial shit like Santa contests. And creepy-as-fuck Santas. And people doing good deeds for other people. And Christmas. And dating. And... flyers.

Huh.

Okay, so possibly I *was* the grumpiest person in O'Leary. I wasn't sure how I felt about that.

I stepped forward in line as Ash came around the counter and stopped by Parker. "Ya got the goods?" he stage whispered.

"Yep." Parker put down his sack and rifled through the contents before pulling out a hunk of red fabric. "And you have *no* idea how hard it was to source a sequoia-sized Santa suit, Ashley Martin. Lay off the Wheaties."

"You're a gem, Parks." Ash winked and smacked Parker's arm lightly. "Gonna go out back and try it on. Be right back."

"'Kay." Parker turned back to me and his smile faltered. "You still mad?"

I blew out a breath. "I'm not *mad*, Parks. Just drop this thing. I'm not a charity case. I have a job I love, a house I love, friends... sort of. It's a fine life. I'm not a sad person." Though possibly a cranky one.

"I know. But your life *could* be even better," he insisted. "And it's not just me who thinks so! The whole town's been talking about it. How you're so grumpy because you must have some great tragedy in your past that broke your heart"—he rolled his eyes—"and how much happier you'd be if you found someone to love."

Motherfucker. "Isn't that delightful? Who died and put *them* in charge of *my* life?"

Parker sighed. "Nobody, obviously. And they're interfering and presumptuous as hell."

"*They*?"

"Fine. *We*," he admitted. "I have become the thing I hated. But... we mean well, dummy. You do *a lot* for this town, and you're... I dunno. You're important to us, man. That's all. And that's what the Santa thing is all about."

The man's eyes shone with kindness, and even I found it hard to be an asshole in the face of his sincerity, but I managed it.

"Parker, don't you have a boyfriend to bother? Shouldn't you scurry along and force your guy into his *own* sequoia-sized red suit? Satisfy your Santa kink that way?"

He tilted his head, exasperated. "It's *not* a kink."

"Mmm. Sure. Far be it from me to yuck your yum, babe. Whatever floats your boat... or, uh... flies your sleigh? But remember charity begins at home."

Parker snorted. "God, you are *such* a jerk. Our own personal Ebenezer Scrooge."

"Accurate."

"I'm afraid that's your first mistake, though," Parker said, his green eyes intent on mine. "Not sure if you've noticed, but people in this town are settling down. Everett and Silas are shacked up. Karen and Mackie have a baby. Hen's making an honest woman of Diane. Cal and Ash are engaged. Jules and Daniel have adopted approximately forty-seven animals. Mitch and Marci finally went public— like a single person in town didn't already know they were together. Constantine and Micah are buying a house in the spring. Dana and Rena are fostering horses. Jamie and I rebuilt the bar, and we're gonna be landlords now."

A small smile danced across his face, like he was so freakin' happy it needed to leak out somehow, and my heart squeezed a tiny bit because—and again, torture couldn't make me say this out loud—he deserved it, and I was damn pleased for him.

"That's lovely for everyone concerned. What's it got to do with you being all up in my business?" I demanded.

"Well, the thing is, there's nothing in the world more irresistible to a person in love than helping a good, deserving friend find a love of their own."

I blinked.

"*You're* the friend," Parker added wryly, like maybe I hadn't made that connection.

God.

"Parker." I coughed. "Did I somehow erroneously and inadvertently indicate that I consider you a friend?"

"*Yup.*" Parker grinned broadly. "That was your *second* mistake."

I opened my mouth to reply when Ash stepped out of the back room clad in head-to-toe red fur, with a giant white beard stuck to his face, and all thought fled my brain, because he was… *wow*.

I'd never understood the concept of a sexy Santa before, and now I could definitively say I *did*, so possibly this day wasn't *all* bad.

"Ho ho ho!" Ash said loudly.

Cal whirled around and his jaw dropped. "Oh. My. *Fu* —" He looked around the bakery packed with patrons, many of whom were kids, and finished lamely, "fresh baked bread."

Ash grinned and wiggled his eyebrows. "Have you been a good boy this year, Caelan?"

Cal snort-giggled—a sound I hadn't thought he was capable of and which was mildly disconcerting—and shook his head helplessly. He kept pushing his lips together, like he was trying to wipe the dopey grin off his face, but it just kept slipping out. "Ashley Martin, you are…"

He broke off, took a step toward Ash, grabbed the man's face with both hands, and yanked him down into a long, thorough kiss that made every person in line, including Lisa "Dragon" Dorian, the town's battle-ax of a librarian, sing a three-part harmony of *"Awww!"*

I did not participate.

"Boom," Parker whispered way too close to my ear. *"Movaries."*

Jesus.

And apparently *no one* was immune to the sight of Ash in the costume, because on the other side of the bakery, someone screamed, "Ohmygod! *Santa!* It's *you!*"

There was the sound of a chair scraping across the floor, a long-suffering *"Hazel Grace!"* and then a half-sized human rushed past Parker and me, barreled around the side of the counter, and threw herself against Ash's legs, knocking him away from Cal.

The kid was *cute*.

I wasn't generally a kid person. I mean, I wasn't a psychopath. I didn't *dislike* children. But I also hadn't spent any time around them since I was a child myself, I had no plans to procreate, and I had zero interest in hearing the trials and tribulations of those who had, so for me to notice that this particular miniature human was *cute* meant she was genuinely, *particularly* cute.

She was all dark curls, tan cheeks, and big brown eyes, and she looked up at Ash with more infectious enthusiasm on her little face than I'd probably ever possessed about anything in my entire life.

"Oh. Wait, no. I ah…" Ash ruffled the girl's hair with one hand and pulled down his beard with the other. "I'm not the real Santa, sweetie. I'm just a, um… helper."

"Oh." The girl took a giant step back and held up her hands. "Shoot. My bad. This is embarrassing."

She sounded five going on fifteen, and I snorted.

So did Cal. "Nah. It's no big. I'm Cal. This is Ashley. Ash helped you and your dad pick out your cookie earlier, remember?"

"Ah, yes. I, um… very much enjoyed it. Your frosting is delicious," she said with such adult over-politeness I had to bite my lip to keep from smiling.

"Thanks." Cal grinned. "You can pick out another one, if it's okay with your dad."

Her smile got even wider as she looked at someone behind me. "Please, Daddy, can I?"

It was none of my business, but that didn't stop me from turning my head toward the little tables by the window to *very strongly encourage* this kid's parent to give her another cookie because she was a fucking ray of sunshine, but when I saw the guy smiling back at her, I froze.

For a minute, I wondered if I'd thought him into existence because, honestly, what were the chances that I'd slipped up and let myself think of Liam for the first time in forever out there on the sidewalk, and then he suddenly appeared, in fucking *O'Leary*, all smiling and sexy in a festive red sweater and jeans that cupped his toned thighs like something out of my personal spank bank?

Slim to none, right?

And yet there he fucking was.

It had been over *five years* since I'd seen that smiling face. Half a decade since I'd felt that silky, dark hair against my fingers and watched that lean, compact body slide across too-soft hotel sheets. A hundred million lifetimes since I'd seen those green eyes—eyes that were infinitely brighter and more beautiful than Parker's poor imitation—widen in pleasure as I made him come and soften with what he'd literally vowed one night, in front of witnesses and a rhinestone-suited minister who looked *nothing* like Elvis, was *love*.

I would have happily gone the rest of my life without seeing any of it—or him—again.

"Last one, Hazel. And what have I told you about accosting strangers?"

"But they're not strangers! They're Cal and Ashley," she said brightly. "They make cookies."

"I have a cookie con artist on my hands," he said dryly, and hearing that teasing voice, all I could think was…

I'm Liam. Liam McKnight. And I'm in town to take pictures of 'fascinating desert landscapes,' but… I'm kinda thinking maybe I found something that fascinates me more.

I swallowed hard, my mouth dry as smoke.

He gave the little girl a lopsided grin, and from the depths of my brain came…

No, you have *the world's most beautiful smile, Gideon Mason. Stop! No tickling! I'm serious, you ass! You know, if I could harness that electricity, I could light up the entire Strip, but I… I think I'd rather keep you all to myself. What do you say?*

"Hey! You were the one who forgot my cookies at home, Daddy!" she giggled.

I sucked in a breath, thrown out of the past and very firmly into the present. Liam was the *father* of a girl who looked to be at least five years old, and very probably more.

And while there were metric shit-tons of things we'd never discussed back in Vegas—all the tiny little details, like whether we liked orange juice or apple juice, or remembered to use the clothes hamper, or meant it when we'd said *forever*—I was realizing that even after all this time, I'd still bought into the fucking romance of the thing. I'd had this idea that, despite him deciding to end us before we'd ever had a chance to *be*, he'd still understood me on the most essential level, just like I'd understood him.

But he'd had a kid and hadn't told me.

Just when I thought I'd already felt as stupid about the whole thing as it was possible to feel, I realized I'd underestimated myself.

I made a choked kind of noise—not loud but pained—and Liam turned his head in concern. His great, green eyes widened.

"Gideon," he breathed.

"Daddy! Can I get a Christmas tree cookie?" Hazel called.

Liam's eyes flickered in her direction, then back to me. "I—"

"Daddy?"

He pushed out a breath. "Stay here," he instructed. He grabbed for my wrist, but stopped a second before contact, like he wasn't sure how I'd react.

I wasn't sure either.

"Please, Gideon. Just... *one* second, okay? I'll be *right* back."

I laughed shortly, and it sounded a little bitter even to my own ears. "I'm not the one with the habit of running away." Though walking away, leaving *him* frustrated and disappointed, was fucking tempting.

Still, when Liam walked over to the counter, I stayed right where I was like my feet had grown roots, staring at the spot where his shoes had been.

"Who the hell is that?" Parker demanded in a hushed voice.

I shook my head.

"Gideon!" He pulled on the sleeve of my jacket. "Who?"

"Fuck." I cleared my throat. "Did you ever have an episode of complete and total madness, Parks?"

"I guess?" His hand tightened on my coat. "Haven't we all?"

"No," I whispered looking up at him suddenly. "No, I don't just mean like you had too many shots of Jäger-meister in college, or you said something to your mom that you didn't really mean, or you ran off to Arizona like a dumbass and didn't tell your boyfriend you'd be back."

"Hey!" Parker grumbled. "*Hurtful.*"

I ignored him. "I mean, have you ever had a moment when you thought... when you thought you really *connected* with someone? Like... I dunno." I shook my head in frus-tration. I was bleating like a broken-hearted asshole, *which I was not*, and yet the words kept spewing forth. "Like there's all the shit that never communicates appropriately from your brain to your mouth when you talk to *other* people, right? But somehow, miraculously, *this one person* got you, so for half a minute you thought maybe all the things you'd believed about yourself and your ability to have a relationship were… were *wrong* because this one person, this *magical person*, existed and understood you?"

Parker's eyes were round. I'd never spoken so many words to him at once, and he probably hadn't thought me capable of it. "I… kinda. Yeah."

I nodded once. "Then imagine how you'd feel if the person you felt that way about just *left* you. Just walked away without a single word, like you'd gotten the whole thing wrong. Like that connection had never existed at all."

Parker scratched his head and the stupid Santa hat shifted back on his blond hair, making him look like a very demented elf. "I, ah… Believe it or not, I know exactly how *that* feels too. But it's never that simple, Gideon. *People* are never that simple."

"In your case, maybe." I set my jaw. "You and Jamie are the exception."

"Or maybe it's *exactly the same,*" he whispered, twisting around to look for Liam and then back to me. "Because fate brought this guy here now, so you could have a second chance to make things right. If you loved him—"

"You're missing the point as usual," I gritted out. "I *thought* it was—" I couldn't bring myself to say love "—*something*, but it was nothing. It was a stupid mistake. A…a one-night stand." That had gotten totally out of hand.

"Whatever you say." Parker sounded positively gleeful. "But you look like you can't decide whether you want to kiss him or beat him to a pulp—"

Not wholly inaccurate.

"—and I've never seen that look on your face ever, so I don't believe you."

I gripped Parker's arm. "Look, before you spin this into some fucking fairy tale, it's not like that," I gritted out. "You can't have a second chance when you never really had a first chance. I don't know why the hell he's here, but I want him *gone*."

"But who *is* he?" Parker demanded. "What's his name? How did you meet him? Is that his kid? When were you together? Why was it only one night? Does he live around here?"

Poor Parker. So adorable. So naive. So fucking *misguided*.

"His name is Liam McKnight," I said, and even saying his name was a kind of magic because my heart clenched with a breathless terror I hadn't felt since the moment I'd walked back to my Vegas hotel suite carrying breakfast and a stupid, overly sentimental rose… and found nothing but a plain, gold ring atop a pile of rumpled sheets. "He's my husband."

Chapter Three

LIAM

I WAS MONUMENTALLY STUPID.

I'd known Gideon Mason for less than an hour before I'd let him press our joined hands against the air-conditioning-cold glass of his hotel room window and fuck me while the lights of the fake Eiffel Tower danced across our skin.

Ten sleepless hours later, we'd watched the sunrise at Valley of Fire Park in utter silence—partly because we'd both lost our voices thanks to too much talking and too-enthusiastic blowjobs, and partly because words would have been redundant.

Twelve hours after that, I'd opened my eyes to Gideon watching me sleep, solid and fierce and real in a way nothing in my life had ever been before. He'd said, "I love you," in his deep, deep voice, with no disclaimer—no, "I think" or "You're gonna say I'm crazy" or "I know it's too soon, but"—and I, Liam McKnight, they guy who wouldn't get a pet hamster or a tattoo because *what if I changed my mind?*, had said "Marry me?" and felt not a single shred of panic once the words were out of my mouth.

Eight more hours, and the surprisingly chilly night air had seeped through our kitschy matching Vegas t-shirts as Gideon and I had walked down to a tiny chapel where a short, blond Elvis with a thick Russian accent formalized our union with a pair of gold rings *that didn't even fit*, because who gave a shit what the ceremony looked like when Gideon's name was already etched on my heart, and we had *forever* to get our rings sized?

Only three days after *that*, I'd finally convinced myself that I *couldn't* take a chance on Gideon and handle all the newfound responsibilities in my life too, and that choice had felt like cutting off a limb.

And for the past five years, despite my best efforts to purge the man from my thoughts, I'd woken up in a panic —not a moment of concern, mind you, but an actual chest-heaving, scalp-sweating, nearly-in-tears, utterly irrational *fit*— multiple times, convinced Gideon had gotten hurt or maimed or killed in a fire, and I'd never know he was gone from this world because I'd lost the right to be informed.

So, how in the *hell* had I thought we'd get through this meeting with air kisses and civilized handshakes and a promise to exchange Christmas cards?

The answer was, I hadn't thought at all.

What the fuck were you supposed to say to the guy you'd walked out on nearly five years ago? Hallmark did *not* make a card for this.

"Daddy? The Christmas tree one?" Hazel blinked up from her perusal of the bakery case, her brown eyes just a tiny bit worried, like she'd noticed my distraction.

I smiled, forcing myself to focus on her. "Sure, Bug. Looks good." To the redhead behind the counter, I said, "Thank you."

The guy waved a dismissive hand. "Always nice to feed

people who appreciate good frosting." He put a beautifully decorated cookie on a plate and handed it down to Hazel. "Enjoy it."

"Thank you, sir," she said politely. She held the plate in two hands as she made her way back to our table by the window and took her seat.

I didn't sit down. Instead I cast a look back at Gideon, who was talking to the guy in the Santa hat like he'd ceased to be aware of my presence. The guy in the hat was cute—his build was lean like mine, but his face was objectively cuter—and the way he was leaning close to Gideon made me wonder if he was a friend or…

None of my business. None. Of. My. Business. Gideon could fuck every guy in town.

He probably had.

And they'd probably loved it every bit as much as I had.

My hands squeezed themselves into fists, and I forced them to unclench.

My *only* business was getting Gideon to sign the paperwork that would cut the final thread tying us together, so we could both move on.

"Hey." I ran a hand over Hazel's curls. "So, remember how I'm here for grown-up stuff?"

She looked up at me, green smeared around her mouth. "Yeah?"

"Well, the person I need to speak to is right over there." I hooked a thumb in Gideon's direction. "I'm going to go have a private *grown-up* conversation while you finish your treat, so don't interrupt unless it's *really* important. Okay?"

Her gaze sharpened with curiosity, and I almost laughed at my rookie mistake. Were any words more compelling to a seven-year-old than *grown-up conversation*?

"While you finish your *second* treat in twenty minutes," I

said pointedly. "Before you've eaten dinner. On this road trip. Where you're missing two days of school." I smiled. "And as someone brilliant once reminded me, *fair is fair.*"

She rolled her eyes and licked her green lips. "Fine. I'm gonna sit here and send my Christmas list to Santa *with my mind.*"

"*Oooh.* You do that."

I turned back to Gideon and didn't allow myself more than a second to take a deep breath and smooth down my sweater before I walked in his direction. *Hard things need to be done quickly,* I reminded myself. *Rip off the Band-Aid.*

Santa Hat watched me approach and shot me a friendly smile over Gideon's shoulder, but Gideon stood stiffly like the only way he could keep from bolting was through not moving at all.

I couldn't help noticing all sorts of shit about him I wished I could ignore. Like the fact that he was taller than I remembered. And that he definitely had more salt in his salt-and-pepper hair than the last time I'd seen him in person. And that the way he held himself—the stiffness to his posture, even when talking to his friend—was more guarded than I remembered.

I wondered if I'd caused that change, and the thought made my chest tight.

I stood near his elbow and cleared my throat. "Uh. Hey."

Gideon didn't turn around.

Off to a great start.

I licked my lips. Did I just drop the words like a bomb and force him to look at me? *Hey! Happy holidays! Feel like signing some divorce papers?*

Did I ask how he'd been, or would that be weird?

Would it be weirder if I *didn't* ask?

Would it be harder to walk away if I knew? Or if I didn't know?

The time we'd spent together five years ago could be measured in *hours*, and yet I couldn't recall a single second of awkwardness; we'd been all-in from the first glance. Now, I couldn't manage to say *hello* without fucking over-thinking it.

Santa Hat grinned widely and reached around Gideon's immobile form to offer his hand. "Hey. I'm Parker Hoffstraeder. Gideon's friend. You're Liam?"

I shook the hand he offered robotically. "Uh. Yeah. Liam McKnight. I'm, um…Gideon's…" I rubbed the back of my neck as I considered how to finish that. *Shit.* I hadn't told anyone about Gideon. Had Gideon told anyone about me? Without seeing his face, I had no clue. So, what the hell did I say?

His friend? His acquaintance? A guy he'd fucked so perfectly that I hadn't had a lover in five goddamn years because Gideon had said he owned my ass, and some part of me still believed him?

Probably not good to start off with that last one.

"You're Gideon's husband!" Parker finished cheerfully. "Yeah, he just told me!"

And *that* seemed to break through Gideon's stony façade at last.

"Shut your damn mouth," he hissed at Parker, looking around the bakery like he wondered who might have overheard.

So, yeah, clearly I was a secret… or *had been*, anyway. At Parker's outburst, practically everyone in the bakery had turned to look at us with expressions of curiosity and surprise.

Gideon grasped my elbow and dragged me to an empty-ish corner in the back of the room. He maneuvered me so I was against the wall and he was blocking me in, like maybe if he couldn't see the dozen people staring at *us*, maybe they couldn't see *him*. Then he lifted his gold-brown eyes to mine.

Shit. *Shit*. I really, *really* should have come up with a script.

"So. Hi," I said. "You look"—I licked my lips—"good."

Understatement.

Also, completely beside the point.

"Liam, what the *fuck* are you doing here?" he demanded.

For a second, I wished I could say anything but what I needed to say. But then I caught sight of Hazel sitting by the window, dragging a finger through the frosting on her cookie and licking it off happily, and I remembered why what *I* wanted didn't matter anymore.

"I had my attorney draw up divorce papers," I said softly, directing my words to the left shoulder seam of Gideon's jacket. "They're out in my car. I just need you to sign them."

"Wait, wait, wait!" Parker leaned around Gideon, interjecting himself into our conversation and looking way too disappointed for a guy who'd just learned Gideon was married in the first place. "Are you sure?"

I looked at Gideon, who just shook his head exasperatedly.

"Uh, yeah. Pretty darn sure," I said.

"But have you considered marriage counseling? Or couples massage? Or… and this is just my personal experience, mind you… but I've found living in the same town to be incredibly helpful." His eyes darted back and forth between us. "Just… don't do anything hasty."

Hasty. Of all the things we'd ever done…

I snorted, and Gideon's darkly amused gaze crashed into mine for half a second of connection before we remembered we weren't supposed to feel that way anymore.

I stared at the ground.

"Liam, you seem like a really nice guy," Parker enthused. "And—"

"Hold up. Based on what?" Gideon demanded, before I could think of a damn thing to say. "The way his ass looks in those jeans? The way he wants to divorce me?"

"No! Just his… his *aura*."

"His aura."

"Yes! Or… whatever you wanna call it." Parker was impatient now. "You know what I mean. *You* married the guy, after all.*"

For one second, I'd swear the air between Gideon and me was a living thing, pulsing with all our unspoken words and unrealized potential.

And then it was gone.

"Parker, you recall my thoughts about you getting involved in my dating life?" Gideon said calmly, not quite looking at Parker but not quite looking at me either.

Parker frowned. "Yeah."

"Then you can imagine how I feel about you interfering in my… my *marriage*." He said it like the word was distasteful.

"But… *Gideon*," Parker said, low and urgent. "*Magical connection*, babe. You said—"

"I *said*, keep your nose out of my business, Parks." Gideon's voice was scary-serious and his eyes were narrowed to slits. "That's what I fucking *said*."

Parker held up his hands in surrender and threw himself into a chair at a nearby table across from an older gentleman.

Gideon turned his head back to look at me, and I could almost swear he was cataloging my features the same way I'd done to him earlier.

"Why now?"

I licked my lips thinking of Hazel, and the riot act my attorney had read me when I'd gone to put a trust in place for her last month and disclosed the minute, inconsequential little detail of my legally binding marriage.

I thought about how lonely I sometimes felt, how unmoored.

I thought briefly of Scott and the fledgling friendship between us, and how maybe that could turn into something uncomplicated that would be, if not wild and crazy and passionate, at least something good enough.

A happy medium was still *happy*, right?

But I didn't say any of that. Instead, I shrugged and said, "It's five years this month. It's been long enough."

The tendons in Gideon's neck stood out for a second before he said, "And you had to hand-deliver these papers? Trekking your ass all the way from... Where are you living now?"

"Uh, still Boston," I whispered, pressing a hand to my stomach. "Just a different area. South of the city."

He nodded once. "And they don't have telephones in Boston? Or mail? FedEx? *Email?*"

"It... I... It's complicated," I said. My gaze inadvertently darted to Hazel again. "Look, can we sit down? I'd love to buy you a cup of coffee and just... explain."

Gideon snorted and lifted his eyes to the ceiling. "The one goddamn person in the universe who *wants* to get me coffee."

"Huh?"

"Nothing." Gideon's voice was hard. "And no, I don't have time for coffee."

"Sure you do!" Parker said from the table. "You were gonna drink coffee anyway, so why not—"

Gideon turned and shut him up with a look. "No fucking coffee."

"Fine," Parker sighed. "But, you know, maybe watch the language? What with the k-i-d around?"

We both ignored him. I was pretty sure Hazel was too far away to hear.

"Okay, how about an early dinner then?" I offered.

"Can't do dinner either. I'm busy."

I frowned. "I'm guessing you couldn't do breakfast tomorrow or brunch on Sunday or teatime a week from next Wednesday either?"

"Nope. I have shifts every day. Firefighter, remember?"

Yeah. I remembered. I bit my lip.

Gideon sighed and ran a hand over his hair. "Just... go get your fucking—"

Parker made an impatient noise, and Gideon glared over his shoulder.

"Go get your papers, Liam," he said, like he was forcing the words out. "I'll sign them right now, and this will all be over and done. We didn't have a big conversation before we got into this mess, and we don't need one to get out of it."

"Fine." I pushed my lips together and told myself I was *not* hurt. It *was* a mess. And getting out of it was *exactly* what I wanted. "We just need a notary to sign off. I'm assuming there's one in town?"

Gideon nodded. "Plenty. Lisa Dorian over at the library is—"

"Gone," Parker interjected.

Gideon turned and frowned. "Gone? Where?"

"She and her sisters went down to the outlets in Cherry

Hill for a long weekend of Christmas shopping. She'll be back Tuesday."

Gideon blinked. "How do you know this shit?" Parker opened his mouth to answer, but Gideon cut him off. "Never mind. I don't care. Rick Chang is probably in his office."

A nervous-looking lady from the table next to Hazel's called out. "I couldn't help overhearing, Gideon, dear. You do remember that little Ross Chang has croup, right? Rick and Kathy took him to the children's hospital over in Syracuse—"

"Fuck," Gideon said under his breath. He closed his eyes tightly, clenched his jaw, and raised his voice as he said. "Right. I forgot. Thank you, Ms. Davenport. For interjecting that helpful information. Into what was supposed to be a private conversation."

"Welcome!" she said without irony. She leaned to the side and told me with a wrinkled nose, "Little Ross is gonna be fine, but Jules said Kathy sounded really shaken up. She took the whole *week* off from the vet clinic, and it's been just devastating to me and to my Macarena."

I nodded slowly. I had no clue who Kathy or Jules or Rick or— *did she say Macarena?*—were, but I understood the feeling.

"When my daughter was three and a bit"—I nodded at Hazel, who'd abandoned all restraint and was now licking her cookie—"she got croup. It was my first time taking her to the ER. I was scared to *death*." I shook my head at the memory. "Parenting is a series of trials by fire."

"Amen," said a frizzy-haired younger woman, seated at a table with a teenaged girl and another girl maybe Hazel's age. She gave me a warm smile and a cheery wave. "Sorry! I couldn't help overhearing either. I'm Jess, and this is my Frannie." She nodded at the little girl. "She's eight."

42

I nodded. "Liam," I said with a tiny wave. "And my daughter is… Hazel."

"She must look like her mother," Jess said. She looked fondly from me to Hazel and back.

I smiled sadly. "She really does."

Jess frowned like she was gonna ask a follow-up, like where Nora *was* exactly, but before she could, the teenager at her table stood up and saved me by handing me a business card.

"Sam Henderson," the girl said. "Best babysitter in town with the most reasonable rates. Call me."

"Oh. Wow. How… entrepreneurial. But I'm only gonna be here for a couple hours, so I'd hate for you to waste a card." I tried to hand it back, but she shook her head.

"Keep it. I have plenty."

Was everyone in this town so… voluntery? I'd lived in my place for almost four years and I knew exactly *one* neighbor. I could not *imagine* introducing myself to a complete stranger, let alone volunteering Hazel's name to anyone I hadn't vetted. But if there was one thing all my travel had taught me, it was how to adapt.

"Right. Awesome." I slid it into my pocket and gave her a polite smile. "Appreciate it."

Gideon frowned at me like I was a specimen under glass or a crossword puzzle clue he couldn't solve.

"What?" I demanded.

"Nothing." He looked away. "What about Jay Turner?" he asked the room at large, since the entire bakery was clearly invested now.

The older gentleman at Parker's table glanced at Parker and shook his head. "Nope. I don't think he'd be up to it, Gideon. Jay's not doing so great. You know how he gets when the weather turns."

"Henry, the man's been complaining about his creaky knees as long as I've known him, and he still managed to win the limbo contest at the freakin' Pumpkin Festival. All he has to do is sign a form."

"But it's icy cold out there! And Jay's in his eighties. You don't mess around with fall risks in your eighties, Gideon." He shook his head. "You know, I broke my leg about a year ago, and to this day my grandson has to—"

"There's not a person in this bakery who's not intimately aware of every detail of your broken leg and how Everett helps you," Gideon snapped. "Paul Fine, then! He's a notary, right?"

Parker nodded once, almost reluctantly. "He is. He's the only other one I can think of."

"And he's in town? Not on vacation? Not sick or arthritic?"

"Uh. Not that I know of." Parker looked around at the other patrons, who all shrugged noncommittally, and added, "But he might not be around! He *is* the head of the town council, so he's *super* busy planning the Santa contest *and* the Light Parade. It's our nondenominational winter holiday festival," he added as an aside to me.

"Oh," I said with a nod. "Nice."

"One of *many* O'Leary festivals," Gideon said, folding his arms over his chest. "*Too* many."

"You know," Cal said pensively from behind the counter. "Somehow I've grown rather fond of them."

"Et tu, Caelan?" Gideon shook his head in disgust.

Cal shrugged, supremely unconcerned. "They're all in good fun—" he began.

"I think someone needs to explain to you people what *fun* looks like," Gideon grumbled. "A clue: a crowd of octogenarians dancing the limbo and a bunch of idiots in Santa hats *isn't it.*"

"Oh, hey, Cal!" Parker said. He snapped his fingers like he'd had a stroke of brilliance. "Why don't you give Paul a call and see if he can come over here to save Gideon and Liam the walk down to find him in the cold." He tilted his head in Hazel's direction meaningfully. "It's after three, and he might be out with Emmylou Harris."

"The singer?" I whispered to Gideon.

"Paul's pug."

"Ah," I said, since this made incrementally more sense.

"Me?" Cal folded his arms over his chest and frowned at Parker. "Why should I call when Gideon could—"

"Because Gideon probably doesn't have Paul's *new cell number*," Parker interrupted. "And you do."

Cal blinked. "I do?"

"Of course you do, Caelan," Henry announced. "I saw him give it to you last week when I was here eating pumpkin pie. Right, Ash?"

"Huh?" Ash looked back and forth from Henry to Parker, a tiny pucker between his brows, then his expression cleared. "Oh! Um. Of course. Last week. When you were here. And there was pie. And the... the phone number. Remember, babe?"

Cal stared at Ash like he didn't recognize him. "But, Ash, you *know* last week we didn't... Oh." Cal looked from Parker to Henry to Gideon. His lips twitched. "*Oh*! Right, right. I remember now! The pie. And the new cell number. Which I have. So, I'll just go..." He hooked a thumb over his shoulder in the direction of the back room. "And, um... call it. And talk to Paul."

"Sweet baby Jesus, I feel myself *aging* over here. Could *someone* call him? Or just give me the number so I can call him myself?" Gideon demanded, and I kinda didn't blame him for losing his patience because the people of O'Leary seemed fucking *weird*. I mean, *nice*. Definitely nice. But… weird.

Cal smiled, grabbed the Santa hat off Ash's head and jammed it on his own. He gave Parker a jaunty salute. "I'm on it."

"Great." Gideon rolled his eyes. "Thank you."

Parker picked up an enormous black sack from the floor. "M'kay. Well. Clearly Caelan has that under control, and I have deliveries to make. Really, *really* nice to meet you, Liam. I'm sure I'll be seeing you around. My boyfriend Jamie and I run the O'Leary Bar and Grille. About two blocks that way." He pointed right. "Come on by and we'll hook you up."

I frowned. "Nice of you to offer, but we'll be leaving just as soon as the papers are signed. Thanks anyway."

Parker smiled. "Remember the offer's open. Later!" He pushed out the door with a jangle of bells.

"You know," I told Gideon, "If the Paul person is close by, we could just walk—"

"Daddy?" Hazel called. "I seem to have a bit of a… situation."

I looked over Gideon's shoulder and found her staring at her two hands, both of which were tinted green. Her face, from her nose to her chin, was one long smear of frosting, and her unbitten cookie sat completely naked on the plate in front of her.

She shrugged sheepishly.

I groaned. Sometimes it felt like my daughter might hit old age before I did. Other times, it felt like she was still a toddler. "Come on. Let's find you a place to wash up."

She got up from the table gingerly and tiptoed toward me. Gideon rubbed a hand over his forehead, and when his brown-gold eyes met mine, it was clear he was trying very hard not to laugh, which was kind of endearing and hot and made my knees weak.

Wow. I really needed to get out of here.

Out of this bakery, out of this *town*, away from this guy and the weird hold he still had on me.

The frizzy-haired lady—*Jess*—reached into her enormous purse and produced a packet of baby wipes. "Here, honey. This'll work."

I took them gratefully and mopped off Hazel's face with the first wipe. Once her face was clean, she stared up at Gideon and let me work on her hands.

"I'm Hazel G. McKnight," she said importantly. "Who are you?"

"Hazel," I sighed, though I wasn't sure what I meant to convey, and both of them ignored me anyway.

Gideon looked down at her. "Gideon P. Mason."

"What's the P for?"

"Hazel Grace," I said more sharply, and she blinked at me innocently.

"Not telling," Gideon said.

Hazel's eyes narrowed. "I don't enjoy secrets."

Gideon snorted and turned an accusing eye on me. "Well, we have that in common."

I clenched my hands into fists around the wet wipe. I hadn't kept secrets... I just hadn't told Hazel or anyone else in my life about Gideon. And I hadn't told Gideon why I needed to leave Vegas. And...

"Not volunteering every single piece of information about yourself isn't the same as keeping secrets," I said. "Mr. Mason doesn't owe you answers."

And I didn't owe him any.

"Welp, bad news," Cal said. He came out of the back room holding his hands up, the very picture of a man who'd given a task his best effort. "Paul's not home. He's in a meeting."

Gideon frowned. "A meeting? What meeting? Where?"

Cal's eyes widened. "And important one. Obviously. He's out for the rest of the day."

"So, there's not a single notary available in this entire town?" I looked at Gideon, who looked even less pleased by this development than I was, if that were possible. "Is there another town nearby?"

"I mean, you *could*... but why bother running all over the place when Paul will be around tomorrow?" Cal said reasonably. "Just stick around for the night, and get it done first thing in the morning."

I sighed and ran a hand over my forehead, pondering. "I guess there's not much difference between spending the night in Syracuse and spending it here."

"But were gonna swim at the pool at the hotel in Syracuse," Hazel reminded me.

"But if you stay in O'Leary, you can have breakfast here. And if you thought the cookies were good, you have no *idea* how good the frosting on my cinnamon rolls is," Cal told Hazel with a wink. "In fact, I can make a special one, just for you, with *mountains* of frosting." And just like that, Hazel was committed.

"I think we should stay here, Daddy," she announced with a decisive nod. "People are so *nice*."

I snorted. "Fine. So, where's the closest hotel?"

"Hotel?" Henry piped up. "Nonsense. Why waste your money on a hotel when Gideon's got that big ol' house of his with all those spare rooms?"

"Absolutely not," Gideon and I said at the same time.

Henry looked back and forth between us, then shrugged. "Suit yourselves."

"Crabapple Bed and Breakfast's two blocks down on

the left. We'll meet back here at nine tomorrow." Gideon nodded once. "Now if you'll excuse me—"

"You mean down the street on the right," Ash said.

Gideon scowled. "No, I mean the left."

"Well now, it depends which way you're coming, doesn't it?" Henry pursed his lips thoughtfully. "Right, left? Could be both, or could be neither."

"It's the left," Gideon insisted. "You walk out the door and take a right—"

"See!" Ash said triumphantly. "It *is* the right!"

"But it's on your left—"

"But it's confusing the way you're explaining it, Gideon," Henry said. "Maybe you should show him the way. Imagine if he took a left and then went right?"

"Why would he—?"

"He'd end up bunking with Julian Ross, and I think Daniel would have a thing or two to say about that." Jess snickered.

"Are you people *trying* to make me insane? It's one street. It's a left and a... I mean, a right and a left!" Gideon said. "Just..." He blew out a harsh breath. "Come on. I will personally escort you to the motherfu—" He looked down at Hazel and swallowed. "The, ah, mother of all bed and breakfasts."

Hazel smiled angelically. "That sounds delightful."

Gideon shook his head but sounded amused when he said, "Come on, Hazel G. McKnight." He put his hand on her little shoulder and led her out of the bakery.

"See you tomorrow, Cal!" she called over her shoulder.

I trailed behind them wondering when my simple plan had gone so wrong...

But I was pretty sure it was the day I'd met Gideon Mason.

Chapter Four

GIDEON

"What do you mean, sold out?" I demanded of the woman in the Santa hat—*another* goddamn Santa hat, like O'Leary had legit taken leave of its collective senses—and the ugliest red and green sweater known to man. "There's no possible way."

Dana, the perky middle-aged blonde who'd been managing the Crabapple for approximately forever screwed her mouth up in a frown.

"Gosh, Gideon, I don't know what to tell you! There's not a single room left until after the first of the year…" She giggled to herself. "No room at the inn! Just like in the Christmas story! Get it?"

"I get it." Liam managed a half-smile.

I didn't bother attempting one.

"*Anyway*," Dana said, sobering when she saw my face. "Parker mentioned your problem to me when he was in here before, but there's nothing I can do! The Scarlet Maple's bogged down with winter weddings, and we're picking up the overflow, as usual. You know, I've always thought it would be so romantic to be married around the holidays. Snowy landscapes, velvet dresses—"

"I do *so* enjoy velvet dresses," Hazel breathed, with what I'd swear was a British accent.

Liam rolled his eyes. I clenched my fists.

There wasn't a damn thing funny about this situation. Seeing Liam earlier had been a shock to my senses I hadn't recovered from. Having him here, in *my* town, interacting with the people I saw on a daily basis, being handsome as hell and adorable as fuck, just prolonged the torture.

Moving to O'Leary had been my fresh start, my way of drawing a line under all the bullshit with Liam in Vegas *and* all the emotional souvenirs I'd brought home. It was a place untainted with memories of me being a disgusting, mopey little angst-nugget, wondering whether I could have saved my two-minute marriage by being a smarter, funnier, more cheerful, generally *better* human.

Now, I'd never walk into *Fanaille* again without thinking of Liam's face in that first second when he'd spotted me. Every time I walked into the fucking Crabapple, I was going to think of his hand on Hazel's shoulder. They'd be back in Boston tomorrow, and I wouldn't be able to stroll down Weaver Street without seeing their ghosts. And it was all Liam's fault.

Was blaming him irrational? Probably.

Did I care? *Hmm*. No.

I was beginning to think Liam and my common sense couldn't coexist in the same place at the same time, whether that place was Las Vegas or O'Leary. Life had taught me to keep my head down and my guard up, but somehow when Liam was around—both of the times Liam had been around—my brain got the two confused. When he was nearby, I couldn't help but *notice* the man, and every twitch of his eyelashes made me weak.

Was this what kryptonite felt like?

"And then, of course, there'll be the crowd in town for the Light Parade a week from tomorrow—" Dana continued.

"What's a Light Parade?" Hazel asked.

Dana smiled down over the desk and her high, blonde ponytail swayed beneath her hat. "It's a festival here in town when *allllll* the shops up and down Weaver Street are lit up for the holidays." She stretched her arm out wide and spoke in a hushed tone. "They have displays in their windows of trees and menorahs and kinaras and diyas and *all* the different kinds of holiday lights. Plus there are toy trains, and nutcrackers, and—"

"And Santa Claus?"

Dana grinned. "Of course, sweetie! And the businesses that don't have stores all set up little booths in the church parking lot. And there's free cocoa, and mince pies, and all the cookies you can eat—"

"Ohhhhh," Hazel breathed. "But like, the *real* Santa? Or… normal humans in red hats?"

Liam caught a breath and held it, but Dana didn't so much as hesitate.

"Well, that's the thing, isn't it? You never really know which is the real Santa. That's where the magic happens."

Hazel nodded solemnly, like Dana had spoken an essential life truth, and despite my mood, I found myself struggling not to smile. Whatever I thought about her dad, the kid was entertaining times a thousand.

"That's gonna be *so* exciting," she said.

Liam squeezed her shoulder gently. "I'm sure it will be, but we'll be back in Massachusetts long before then. You have school, remember?"

"For only two more days until winter break! We could—"

"We could *not*," Liam said with finality. "End of story."

Hazel sighed.

"That's a shame! We get lots of people who come to town just to enjoy the day and take pictures," Dana said.

"My dad takes pictures," Hazel told her new best friend. "They're even in magazines. And he's making a book."

"That right?" Dana said, cocking her head. "A professional photographer?"

Liam nodded uncomfortably. "I do contract work for a couple of media outlets. You know, background photos, news photos. Nothing major."

"Shut up. You're talented as hell." I wasn't sure where those words had come from—I sure as heck hadn't made a conscious decision to say them—but I folded my arms over my chest and stared Liam down because I stood by them.

He'd shown me a few of his pieces back in Vegas, and it was possibly *possible* that one time in a weak moment, I'd gotten drunk and googled his work, and I could say for certain his modesty was ridiculous.

I had serious issues with Liam as a person and Liam as a *partner*, but if a two-dimensional picture could make a man like *me* feel emotions, it was a fucking exceptional picture.

Liam blinked. "Oh. Well. I—" He swallowed. "Thanks."

"And do you do *portraits*?" Dana asked avidly.

"Well. Not usually—"

"But you did portraits of me," Hazel argued. To Dana, she said, "I was wearing a dress with *silk roses*. It's hanging in our *living room*."

Dana nodded, suitably impressed.

Liam rubbed the back of his neck. "This isn't gonna

find us a place to stay tonight, unfortunately. Is there another hotel nearby?"

"I mean, there's the campground," Dana said dubiously, and for good reason since it was going to freeze again tonight.

"Camping!" Hazel turned wide eyes on her father and then up at me. "I've always wanted to go camping!"

"Not in winter," Liam said in a tone that brooked no argument.

Hazel sighed.

So did I. There weren't a lot of options left, and I was more than a little annoyed that this had somehow become my problem.

"Motel over in Rushton's not ideal, but it'll have to do," I said. "You can follow me—"

"You can't!" Dana blurted. "They have a… a rat problem."

"Rats?" Liam said, looking at me like maybe he'd misunderstood.

"Mmm. *Huge* ones. With big, sharp *teeth*." Dana held up two curved fingers in front of her mouth. "*Everybody's* been talking about it."

"Have they?" I narrowed my eyes. "I haven't heard a word."

"Well, I mean everybody who's involved in, ah… lodging and hospitality specifically," Dana explained.

"Well, I think the secret might have spread to the general public if there were *giant rats*—" I began, but Hazel stopped me with a tug on the hem of my jacket.

"I *really* dislike like rats," she whispered. "I also dislike the *possibility* of rats."

I looked at Liam, who shook his head. "Yeah, the motel's a no-go. *Someone* will be up all night. And if she's up, I'll be up."

"Shi…Uh. *Sugarplums*. Well, I don't know where else." I frowned.

"Hey, Gideon," Dana interrupted. "You've got that big old house. Don't *you* have a place your…*friend* can stay?"

"We're not friends," Liam and I said at the same time.

Our eyes met, he nodded once, and I knew he got it too. *Friend*ship implied a connection that was too small for the way we'd been together, and too big for the total lack of communication since the day he'd left me.

Dana shrugged. "Maybe try Parker and Jamie's place across the street? They don't have a tenant for the apartments over the Bar and Grille, last I checked."

———

"Fumigating," I repeated, staring at the redhead on the other side of the bar. "Jamie, how in holy"—I glanced down at Hazel, who was perched on a stool, thumping the bar gently with the toe of her shoe and eating a cheeseburger Jamie had made her —"holy *hot chocolate* can you have termites when you only finished building this place a few months ago?"

"Ah… well." Jamie rubbed the back of his neck and freckles stood out beneath his pink cheeks. "Termites are really unpredictable."

"Unpredictable?" Liam said in confusion. "Are they?"

"Mmm. Like, looking back, on the, uh, situation, I feel like one minute things were perfectly fine? And then all of a sudden… *infestation*." He threw up his hands in an exaggerated motion that I'd swear was *way* too perky for Jameson Burke, unless living with Parker was getting to him. "Parks and I would love to help you out, but I'd hate for you to inhale the poison or come dropping through the floor. So…"

All four of us glanced uneasily at the ceiling.

"No," Liam said. "Definitely not."

"You know, Parker didn't mention anything about this earlier today." I narrowed my eyes.

"Didn't he?" Jamie's smile was bland. "Hmm. He probably didn't want to worry you."

"Ah. Of course." I folded my arms over my chest. "He's such a giver."

Giver of *headaches and really shitty life advice.*

"And he's so busy organizing the Santa thing," Jamie continued. "Been out delivering costumes all day. I only saw him for half a second when he came to deliver mine."

"God, you too? Is anyone *not* dressing up as Santa?" Was there anyone *safe* in all of O'Leary?

"Not my idea. You might say Parks voluntold me I'd be taking part."

"You sound devastated," I said wryly.

Jamie grinned mischievously. "What can I say? The job comes with compensation. Really, really lovable compensation."

I rolled my eyes.

"If you're a Santa," Hazel asked, "where's your hat?"

"Over there." Jamie nodded to a folded pile of red velvet on the bar next to the cash register. "My plan is to be a covert kind of Santa, though." He gave Hazel a teasing wink that made her laugh. "A Secret Agent Santa."

"So... Parker was here," I confirmed, a conspiracy theory beginning to take root in my mind.

"Of course he was here." Jamie gave me a steady look. "He co-owns this bar. *Duh*."

"Hmm. And he didn't happen to talk about *me* did he?"

"Gideon, believe it or not, our conversations are almost *never* about you." Jamie grinned, and I noticed he hadn't actually said *no*. "Except… remember that time you were flirting with Parker last spring, and I got insanely jealous? You *were* mentioned that time."

Three sets of eyes landed on my face, and I tried hard not to notice the way Liam's cheeks turned pink.

"*I* flirted with Parker? Pretty sure you're mistaken."

"Sure I am," Jamie agreed easily. "You'd never interfere in anyone's relationship that way, right? Ha. *Me neither.* Anyway! Let's think of who might have extra room." Jamie tapped his lip thoughtfully. "Hmmm. Sam's staying out at Angela's part time now, so that won't work. Con and Micah only have the one bedroom. Cal and Ash's spare room is *tiny…*"

Liam sighed. "It's fine. Thanks anyway. We'll just drive—"

"Oh, hey!" Jamie said, his brown eyes unnaturally wide. "Gideon, don't *you* have a whole bunch of extra room at your place?"

Subtle as a fucking sledgehammer.

"Thanks for the burger, *Secret Agent Santa*," I said through clenched teeth. I tossed a twenty-dollar bill on the bar. "You ready, Hazel Grace?"

She nodded and grabbed my hand to jump down from the bar stool.

"You could always check with Jules and Daniel!" Jamie called after us. "The apartment above the vet clinic might be free!"

———

"Snakes." I eyed the oversized blond from across the table at Goode's Diner. "Really."

Liam and I were squashed into one side of a tiny booth, and even though we were making a concerted effort not to touch, the man smelled more delicious than anything on Goode's menu.

Fortunately, the web of bullshit Daniel was spinning made a half-decent distraction.

"Yep. Freakiest thing. This giant boa constrictor got into the…" Daniel waved a finger at the ceiling. "What do you call it?"

"Heating ducts?" Liam suggested.

Daniel pointed at him excitedly. "Exactly. *Yes.* Heating ducts. And then, um… it laid eggs. And they hatched. And now we're overrun." He shrugged broadly. "Too bad, because I'd've loved to offer you two a place to stay, Liam."

Liam nodded, and his arm rubbed against mine. Even through his sweater and my jacket, I was hyper aware of the heat of his skin.

Have you ever been attracted to someone you have every reason to dislike?

Let me give you the CliffsNotes. *It fucking sucked.* Possibly even more than having snakes in your heating ducts.

Hazel looked up from her ice cream sundae and frowned at the man beside her. "But boa constrictors are a type of snake that gives birth to live babies. I saw it on a documentary once."

"Oh, did I say a boa constrictor?" Daniel scratched his cheek with one finger. "Silly me. I meant a… um…viper?" He took a sip of his coffee, apparently unconcerned.

"*Wait.* Wait wait wait," Liam said, shaking his head. "You have a venomous snake in your HVAC—"

"Multiple venomous snakes," I corrected helpfully.

"Yes! Thank you." Liam nodded once in my direction. "*Multiple* venomous snakes in your HVAC system? That's… unbelievable."

"Literally," I said. But then again, Daniel was a novelist, so this was hardly surprising.

Daniel nodded solemnly. "I can scarcely believe it myself. But then, truth is stranger than fiction, right?"

"Not always," I said darkly.

The diner door opened, a black-haired man strolled in, and I lifted a hand in greeting. "Jules! Come join us. We were just talking about you and your problem."

"*Ah, crap*," Daniel said under his breath.

"Hey, guys!" Julian unwound the scarf from his neck and leaned over Hazel's head to give his boyfriend a kiss. He smiled broadly at Liam. "You must be Gideon's hus… guest. His guest."

"Nice save, baby," Daniel said approvingly. "Did you get Parker's text?"

"Sure did!" Julian smiled harder. "Yeah, Parker told me about your situation. Gosh darn it, I would just love to have you stay at our apartment, if not for our devastating lizard problem!"

"Lizards?" Liam said, looking from Julian to Daniel. "I thought you said *vipers*."

"Vipers?" Julian said, staring at Daniel in horror. "What?"

Daniel held out a hand and Julian came around the far side of the booth to perch on Daniel's knee.

"*Snakes*, Jules. It was definitely *snakes*," Daniel insisted.

"Are you sure? Because I really thought—"

Daniel leaned across the table toward Liam and me, "So sad. Denial is a powerful thing. Surely you remember, babe. The viper that got loose. And laid eggs."

Julian's lips pursed and he was visibly *vibrating*, probably with the need to insert some obscure animal fact that would make this improbable tale *impossible*, but instead he nodded slowly. "That's... yes. Silly me. *Vipers in the heating duct.* It slipped my mind."

"So have you called someone else? Animal control? Or the police?" From the look on his face, Liam obviously suspected everyone in O'Leary was *insane*, rather than just insanely meddlesome.

"Obviously." Daniel squirmed in his seat. "As any reasonable people would."

"And?"

"And what?" he hedged.

"*And* what did they tell you to do?" Liam said impatiently. "How will they get rid of the snakes?"

"Oh, that." Daniel hesitated. He looked blankly at Jules, Jules looked blankly back at him. "Julian tells the story better than I can. Fill them in, baby."

I recognized the moment when Julian found himself trapped and decided to go all-in. "They suggested we, um." He coughed gently. "Charm them out."

"Charm them? Like with *music*?" Hazel's eyes were wide.

"Mmhmm. So Daniel's learning to play the pan flute." He coughed again. "Those snakes will be gone... any day now."

"I'd hate to hear what *un*reasonable people would do," I said to no one in particular.

Daniel buried his face in Julian's back and his whole body shook. Julian patted his arm comfortingly. "He gets embarrassed," Julian whispered to Liam and me. "His flute playing is..." He tilted his hand from side to side. "At best."

"Hey!" Daniel's face emerged from behind Julian, his eyes wet and his cheeks red. "I'll have you know I have never had a complaint about my flute playing! Admittedly, I've only ever played the one flute."

"It's *not* about the number of flutes you play," Julian said solemnly. "It's about how often you practice."

Daniel poked Julian in the ribs, making him laugh. "At least *I* can read *emojis* in *text messages!*"

"Are we still talking about snakes?" Hazel wanted to know.

"As much as we ever were," I told her dryly. To Daniel and Julian, I suggested, "Maybe you should run along and play Pied Piper now?"

"Good idea," Daniel agreed, pushing Julian to his feet. "Just… to avert a public health situation. Hey, Gideon, you have plenty of room in that big, old house of yours. Couldn't they stay—"

"*No,*" I said shortly.

"Sorry, guys," Jules said, looking anything but. "Um. If you need a place to stay, maybe check with Silas and Everett? Ev has an art studio over their garage he might let you use!"

"Who are Everett and Silas?" Liam asked, looking tired and more than a little shell-shocked after Julian and Daniel left. "And what are the chances they're having a plague of locusts? Or a sewage leak? Or hosting a convention of platypuses?"

"High," I snorted. "Very high."

"Is everyone around here just super unhelpful to newcomers?" Liam demanded. "I don't get it."

"No! No, not at all." I paused and thought about it. "Okay, yes, sometimes. But with you, it's more like they're trying to ensure you never leave O'Leary."

Liam's eyes widened.

"No, no. Not in a serial killer way. More like… more like… think of the cheesiest rom com you've ever watched and multiply it by a dozen Santa wannabes."

"Oh-kayyyy?"

"See, if there's no place in town for you two to stay, you'll have to stay with me, right?"

"Or sleep in the car. Or head back to Syracuse," Liam said slowly. "Or a thousand other things."

"Stop talking sense, Liam. This is O'Leary. Around here, logic is always the last resort."

He chuckled reluctantly. "Okay, fine. So I stay with you. Because there's *literally* no other option. And?"

"And... *boom*. Movaries."

Liam blinked. "What?"

I shifted on the seat and waved a hand in the air. "Clearly the intense attraction between us will be too much to resist and we'll be fu"—I glanced at Hazel, wondering if maybe Parker was right about my foul language, and swallowed—"*fa la la-ing* before the night is out."

I rolled my eyes like the notion was outrageous, but... every fucking time the guy moved, all I could smell was his cologne—something orangey and spicy—and something vanilla too, like residual frosting. And it was a measure of how far I'd sunk over the past few hours that despite our whole shitty history and the kid sneaking glances at us from across the table, I was sorely tempted to lick him just to see if he tasted as good as he smelled.

"Wow," Liam said. His nose wrinkled and his eyes danced. "*Fa la la-ing*? You have a gift for euphemisms."

I shrugged. "I swear like a trucker. I'm trying to control myself."

"Right, so." He ran a hand over his forehead tiredly. "The people of your town are trying to find you someone to *fa la la* with? That's... odd, no? Have you already *fa la la-ed* the entire local populace, and they need to import new people?"

I dug my fingers into my knee under the tabletop. The note of jealousy in his voice was probably my own wishful thinking, but the way the idea made my cock twitch was very, very real.

"I'm not a guy who talks about how many people he's *fa la la-ed*, Liam." Especially when the number was mortifyingly low over the past five years. "Besides, it's much more insidious than that. See, once we've... *fa la la-ed*, it's just a hop skip and a jump to us forgetting our history, losing our minds, and falling for each other again. Then someone will be repainting the Welcome to O'Leary sign to say Population 1076."

"That's..." He paused and blinked. "Okay, I don't even know what that is. Besides ridiculous. Obviously."

"Absurd," I agreed.

Liam cleared his throat and didn't look at me. "Hazel, two more bites of ice cream and we've gotta go. It's already dark outside, and we've got a long drive to find a hotel."

Hazel paused, spoon halfway to her mouth, and stared at him in horror. "What? But no! Daddy, we said we'd stay! I'm going to eat a cinnamon roll with a *mountain of frosting* for breakfast."

"You heard the part where no one has a place for us to stay, right?" He huffed out a breath. "If we leave right now, you can still have your cinnamon roll in the morning. We have to come back here tomorrow anyway to finish up our business." Liam pushed to his feet and grabbed his wallet out of his pocket.

"But, Daddy!" she whined.

"Hazel," he said, clearly at the end of his patience. "*Enough.* We're leaving. Now."

It hit me again, just like it had hit me back at the bakery when he was talking about croup and hospitals, that it must be a fucking hard thing to parent a kid. Just the stamina required to resist those eyes was a lot.

"But..." Hazel turned those giant, weaponized brown

eyes on me. "Gideon, can't we stay with you? In one of your spare bedrooms? In your big old house?"

She batted her eyelashes, stuck out her lower lip, and clasped her hands—one of which was still wrapped around her drippy spoon—beneath her chin. It was hilarious, aggravating, and charming all at once. *Irresistible*, I would have said, but in truth I could resist it.

"No, we can*not*. And since when do you invite yourself places?" Liam left some cash on the table. "There'll still be plenty of sugar left in this town *tomorrow* when we come back. Get moving."

Liam looked… truly drained. Worn thin. Still gorgeous, because life would be too easy if I could find a way to turn off this unwelcome attraction. But those pretty green eyes used to be carefree, bubbling over with enthusiasm, and now they looked defeated, which was unacceptable.

Yeah, Liam was *not* my responsibility, and yeah, I was royally *pissed* at the whole situation—at him for leaving *and* at him for coming back, at myself for still giving a shit, at the town for their conniving—but it didn't seem to matter. I couldn't see him truly distressed and just… ignore it.

Unlike Hazel's pout, sad Liam *was* irresistible.

"You *should* stay at my house," I announced.

Liam looked at me, a tiny line between his eyes. "But you *just* told me—"

"I told you my so-called friends were trying to manipulate us into that situation," I agreed. "But they don't know our history. They don't get how impossible it all is. Stay at the house."

"We can't put you out."

"Liam." I stood and put a hand on his shoulder, squeezing lightly. "Ask anyone in this town and you'll learn I rarely do anything that will put me out. It *is* a big old house. I have two spare rooms—plus a bedroom that's a gym, and one that's an office. There'll be no chance of accidental *fa la la-ing*. Everything will be fine." I smirked. "Unless you think you're incapable of resisting my charms."

"*That* won't be a problem," he said, folding his arms over his chest. "But—"

"The Camden Road is dangerous after dark," I reminded him. "Lots of twists and turns and switchbacks between here and Syracuse."

He hesitated, and in his fatigued state, I could almost see the wheels turning in his brain, remembering the road and weighing that discomfort against the discomfort of staying with me. The shoulder beneath my hand was so tense, it was a wonder he didn't pop like a balloon and fly into a million pieces.

Finally, he relented with a nod.

"Excellent!" Hazel dropped her spoon into her empty dish with a clatter, wiped her mouth, and jumped out of the booth. "Let's go!"

At least one of us was looking forward to the evening.

Chapter Five

GIDEON

I COLLECTED MY TRUCK AT THE FIREHOUSE, AND LIAM and Hazel followed me the half mile home. As we drove up the long, sloping driveway from the street, I felt my stomach flip with nerves. I wondered whether I had any food in the house and whether there were sheets on the beds, and then I mentally slapped myself for becoming my fucking *mother.*

Since when did I give a shit what anyone thought?

Liam and Hazel were staying with me because I was a sap, and they were desperate. At least I didn't have rats. Or snakes. Just a bunch of nosy neighbors with a hard-on for Christmas, and a shit-for-brains friend hell-bent on matchmaking, and a soon-to-be ex-husband who was the single sexiest thing I'd ever seen in my entire lifetime.

What could go wrong?

Liam pulled up alongside me in front of the detached garage and for a second he and Hazel sat there staring at the massive, cream-colored colonial with its sage-green shutters, glowing in the light that spilled from the wide front porch.

Hazel opened her door first. "Your house is *amazing!*"

She scampered up the path to the front door while Liam got a truly excessive number of suitcases out of the trunk. But instead of following Hazel, he stood and stared at the house some more, like he wasn't quite sure whether to smile or frown.

"What?" I demanded.

"Nothing. Just… it's huge. And gorgeous. I just sorta figured you'd have something more minimalist. Practical."

It bothered me that he thought he knew me, even after all this time.

It bothered me more that he was right.

"You've seen O'Leary, right? You think this metropolis runs to modern architecture?" I snorted. "I got this for a steal and fixed it up, which *is* practical. Besides," I said, shouldering two of his bags, "if I *always* made practical decisions, you wouldn't be here, would you?"

Liam made a sound like I'd startled a laugh out of him and followed me inside.

"There's no table in your dining room," Hazel informed me when we hit the front hall, and my gaze followed the direction of her pointing finger to a room with immaculate floors, a beautiful chandelier, and no furniture whatsoever.

"Isn't there?" I pretended to look around. "Shoot. It must've walked off again."

"But *why* is there no table?"

"Hazel," Liam said tiredly. "Stop with the twenty questions—"

"Chill, Liam. She can ask whatever she likes. Doesn't mean I'll answer it." To her, I added, "I don't need a table since I generally don't have anyone over for dinner. You're the exception."

"But." She frowned. "Where did you and your family

eat on Thanksgiving? Or do you choose not to celebrate for political reasons?"

For… political reasons?

I looked at Liam who gave an exaggerated shrug that said I'd made my bed and now I could lie in it.

"My parents and my sister and brother ate dinner at my parents' house, which is a few hours from here. I'm a firefighter and I was on duty that day, so I ate at work."

"Did you have *turkey*?"

"I did. And potatoes, which are better than turkey."

"Agreed," she said after a moment's thought. "And pie?"

"Of course, pie. There are no holidays without pie."

"Or cake."

"Mmmm. I'm gonna disagree with you there," I said, folding my arms over my chest. "Pie is the superior dessert."

She pondered this, then nodded. "Apple pie or pumpkin?"

"Apple."

"Whipped cream or ice cream?"

"Both."

"Chocolate pie or pecan?"

"I already told you, apple. I'm a one pie kinda guy."

"Do you celebrate Christmas?"

I shrugged. "I might go see my family, and I always buy presents for my nephews. Is that celebrating?"

"Why don't you have any Christmas decorations?"

"Because it's annoying to put them up, annoying to take them down, dangerous to have them around, and they're essentially meaningless?"

"Dangerous how?"

"Because some of them can start fires and others can make fires *worse*."

She lifted an eyebrow. "If they're so dangerous, why do lots of people still put them up?"

"Because lots of people do foolish things?"

"But maybe you could have *some* decorations that *aren't* dangerous."

I shook my head. "Christmas decorations are a slippery slope, kid. One minute you're hanging a stocking, the next minute you've got an inflatable sleigh on your front lawn."

"What's your middle name?"

I grinned. "Still not telling."

"Hmm. Why don't you have friends over for dinner?"

"Back to that?" I shrugged again. "Maybe because people ask too many questions?"

She grinned. "I like you."

"I like you too." I tugged gently on one of her curls. "And since you have such great taste, you get to pick which bedroom you want first."

We carted the luggage upstairs, where Hazel picked the guest room she liked best and immediately began unpacking a bunch of toys like she'd be staying for a while. Meanwhile, Liam followed me back down to the kitchen.

"Beer?" I offered. Liam shook his head, but I popped the top on a Sam Adams because when you were forced to spend time with the guy you didn't want to like and sort of reluctantly did, a guy whose hair made you want to touch it and whose smile made you want to smile, a guy who was possibly the one great love of your life, *and* the person who'd fucked off and crushed you, *and* the man you were going to divorce in the morning, alcohol was sort of required.

"Chicken and peppers alright for you and me?" I asked, grabbing the pasta pot from the drawer by the stove.

"Yeah, fine. *Shit*. I didn't think." Liam pushed the hair

off his forehead. He still looked exhausted. "Hazel had her burger, but I could have gotten takeout for us—"

"In this town?" I smirked. "Takeout means pizza, and even then, you have to order it before seven. Besides, it's fine. I like cooking."

"Hmm," he said. "I didn't know that. I also didn't know your favorite pie was apple."

"I don't expect you to know shit. The sum total of all the things we don't know about each other is probably twenty times the things we do know, right? Or *knew*. We're basically strangers."

Which was absolutely true… and also the world's biggest lie.

I got out all the ingredients for the chicken and a salad to go with it, and Liam immediately started washing and chopping produce on the opposite side of my center island. Meanwhile, Hazel settled on the rug in the living room with crayons and paper, humming quietly to herself.

I'd expected it to be weird. Uncomfortable. But it was… companionable.

And yeah, weird and uncomfortable *because* it was so companionable.

I could count on one hand the number of people who'd been out here over the years—Parker, when he'd brought me some old bookcases he and Jamie were clearing out of their house, and my parents when they'd stopped by on their way to a Jets-Bills game last winter, just long enough for my dad to approve the floors I'd refinished and my mom to offer me every knickknack in her home to "liven up the place."

If anyone had asked, I'd have said that had been *plenty* of visitors because I valued my solitude.

But now, looking at Hazel sprawled on the rug, and

listening to Liam as he picked up Hazel's tune—which I now recognized as a Christmas carol—it was... nice.

I mean, I didn't hate it.

"*Oh my Goddddd!*" Hazel's scream echoed through the downstairs and Liam dropped his knife to the counter with a clatter, but when she came running into the room a second later, she seemed fine.

The ball of orange-yellow fur in her arms, however, looked a bit harried.

"Daddy! It's a *kitten*!"

Liam looked at the cat strangely. "So it is."

"That's Fia," I said. "She's my buddy. I forgot to mention her when you got here."

"I *adore* cats," Hazel said. "Can I play with her?"

"Sure. If she'll let you."

Liam held out a hand for her to sniff and she hissed.

"Gah!" He pulled back sharply.

"She doesn't like you, Daddy."

"She doesn't like strangers and doesn't believe in being polite for the sake of politeness," I said. She was a lot like me that way.

But of course she let *Hazel* pet her, and even laid down on the rug and curled herself around Hazel's waist when she went back to coloring pictures. Liam watched them with narrowed green eyes.

"So, it's not *all* strangers she has a problem with. I think you've been showing the cat my picture and training her to attack," Liam said.

"You caught me. It was hard to do, considering I don't have a single picture of you, but I used my psychic abilities"—I tapped a hand to my temple—"and beamed your image into her brain. Pleased to see it worked."

"You don't have pictures?" He frowned. "Hmm."

"What? You thought I'd saved those cheesy pics of you,

me, and Russian Elvis? That maybe I cry myself to sleep over them every night? Please," I snorted. "Sorry to disappoint. I assume housekeeping trashed them along with all the other crap we left behind."

In fact, I *had* kept one tiny souvenir from that weekend, one symbol of my naive optimism and my stupidity. The shiny gold ring I'd given Liam—the ring he'd left behind—sat in my drawer upstairs, where I could take it out and look at it if I were ever again tempted to do something as epically idiotic as falling in love.

I was happy to say I'd almost forgotten its existence… until now.

Liam cleared his throat and went back to his work, slicing peppers into ever-tinier slices. "So, you saved the cat from a fire, huh?"

"What?" My mind was two thousand miles away, in a hotel suite in Vegas.

"Your cat. I, uh… googled you earlier this week, and I saw the cutest picture from a couple months ago of you cuddling a cat that looked just like Fia, while dressed in all your fire gear like you were Mr. September in the Firefighters of New York calendar. The, uh, caption said you were in O'Leary, New York. That's how I first tracked you down."

"Figures. That photo is the bane of my existence," I said, rolling my eyes. "Brings me nothing but shit."

I hadn't really considered what I was saying until I'd said it. I'd *meant* that I'd heard enough trash-talking about my sex-symbol status from the other guys at the station—and from Parker—to last a lifetime. But Liam's eyes went soft and sad in misunderstanding, and I didn't know if it would be better or worse to correct him because I had no freakin' clue what *better* and *worse* even looked like in this situation.

I'd been worried about the man haunting my *town*, but now he was in my damn *house*. I'd said we weren't friends, but I found it hard to stay mad at him—which was fucking weird, since I had no problem being an asshole to basically everyone else in the world. I was also really fucking tired because I'd been awake for over twenty-four hours, but I felt like I'd been juiced with a live wire.

So I concentrated on cutting up chicken and said nothing.

"So Fia's an interesting name," he ventured after a minute. "Is it Italian?"

"Close. It's Latin. It means fiery. Seemed like her mama and her litter mates abandoned her during the fire, and I couldn't just leave her there, so." I shrugged, uncomfortable. "She came home with me."

"That's really adorable. The name, the story."

"Yeah, well." I turned away to dump the cut-up chicken into a pan. "I had a piece of debris fall on my head during that fire, so I wasn't thinking clearly."

"How badly were you hurt?" Liam's voice had lost all trace of humor, and I turned back to him with a frown.

"Not bad. Just a knock on the head."

"What did the doctor say?" he demanded.

"I didn't see a doctor. What for?"

"Because you don't take chances with knocks on the head, dummy. You get X-rays"—he cast his pretty green eyes to the ceiling—"because it might look like there's no injury on the surface, but something could have gotten messed up underneath."

He was... *worried*? How weird was that? But my chest tightened because it was also kind of sweet. Made it harder than usual to stare him down and achieve my usual sarcastic tone... but I did it.

"I'm touched, Liam, but clearly I managed to survive without your input."

I turned back to stir the chicken and he fell silent. With nothing to focus on but the sounds of Liam chop-chop-chopping and Hazel talking softly to the cat, I felt like a jerk… possibly because I was.

"I just meant adopting her was a moment of weakness," I caved and explained. "You know, from the head injury? It was a joke."

Liam's chopping paused. "Since when is it a 'moment of weakness' to feel a basic human emotion and act on it?"

The air between us pulsed with the truth we both recognized.

Since five years ago this month.

"Look." Liam set down the knife with a *thunk*. "Let's clear the air here. Five years ago, I had to do one of the hardest things I've ever done. But it wasn't because—"

I turned around again, brandishing my spoon like a weapon. "*Whoa, whoa, whoa.* Have I in any way indicated that I give a shit?"

Liam's jaw clenched. "Yeah, you kinda have."

"Well, I don't. I told you earlier today, I'm not interested in explanations or long, heartfelt stories. I don't need for you and me to be all kumbaya, okay? You left, and it was shitty. It hurt my tiny feels, I admit it. But that was *five years ago*. I'm over it. I've *been* over it. I see absolutely no need to rehash it."

I literally could not think of anything worse than Liam explaining what had happened five years ago. How he'd woken up to realize what a huge mistake we'd made, how he'd chosen to leave without a word of explanation because he was too horrified to explain it to my face. Not to *mention* the whole secondary issue of him having had a *child* at the time. One he hadn't even mentioned to me.

Jesus fuck no. I'd rather pose for a hundred shirtless pictures with kittens. I'd rather let the entire town of O'Leary set me up on dates. I'd rather dress up as Santa and pass out Joe's fucking flyers on Weaver Street.

Because after Liam explained, what would he do? Say he wished he'd handled things better, but how ultimately it had worked out for the best? And then... was I supposed to laugh and smile and say no hard feelings? Fuck that. I wasn't built for niceties. The very idea made me want to hiss like Fia.

Liam McKnight was gorgeous and kind and funny and sexy as hell—a fucking human flame that could light the darkest night, burn away the deepest chill. But when we came together? It was an uncontrolled blaze.

I didn't hate the man. Exactly the opposite. And that made me remember how vulnerable I was.

"But—"

"But nothing. Subject closed. And I'm not kidding, Liam. We'll talk about the weather and...and... *pie flavors* for the rest of the evening, and we'll sign the paperwork tomorrow, and it'll be done. You go your way, I'll go mine."

Liam clenched his teeth. "You're a fu—*fa la la-ing* pain in the posterior, you know that?"

"Many men have said so."

"Ugh." Liam rolled his eyes. "Fine. Have it your way." I could almost swear he muttered something under his breath about "air kisses and handshakes," but he didn't push the issue, so I didn't call him on it.

I pulled another beer from the fridge and tipped it in Liam's direction. This time he took it.

"So. Photography business going well?"

My small talk ability was basically non-existent and —*shocker!*—Liam noticed. His eyebrow lifted mockingly.

"Pretty sure this isn't pie flavors."

"From what I remember it's your favorite conversation topic in the world, so not exactly a conversational minefield either, is it?" I frowned. "Or *is* it?"

"Nah." He waved a hand, but his smile was gone. "Photography's fine. Keeps the lights on. So far."

"Wow. Don't hurt yourself with that enthusiasm. I seem to remember you wanting to permanently mount a camera to your hand."

In fact, that excitement had been one of the first things that had drawn me to him... but that *was* a conversational minefield, so I steered clear.

"I love photography. Just, like most things, it loses some of its shine when you're doing it for *work*. Gotta take all the jobs that come your way, even the ones that don't *speak to your muse*." His mouth twisted into a self-mocking smile. "Welcome to adulthood, right?"

"I don't know. Is adulthood supposed to be misery?"

"It's not misery, it's compromise. I'm focusing on the steady paycheck, so I can pay for college and retirement and all that. Oh, life insurance too." He laughed shortly. "One of those things you don't think about until it's too late."

"But there's gotta be a place where what you want to do and what you *have* to do overlap, right? A happy medium? A thing you enjoy doing that will also make you money?"

He snorted. "A happy medium."

"What? It's a thing."

"I know, I know. Just, earlier today I was thinking..." He broke off with a shake of his head. "Never mind. Yeah, you're right. It would be nice to find a happy medium somehow."

"Hazel said you were working on a book."

"Uh. Yeah. Just an idea I'm working on in my copious

spare time." He lifted a shoulder. "More of a pipe dream for now."

He sounded a little dubious, which was totally unlike the Liam I remembered, and it made me a little sad.

It was tempting to think he'd left that morning back in Vegas and sort of ridden off into a happy sunrise, but that wasn't true, just like it wasn't true that I'd been miserable every minute we'd been apart, or that we'd have *definitely* been happier if he'd stayed.

It was hard to blame someone for not having faith in *us* when it sounded like he didn't have much faith in *himself* anymore.

"Hey, since when do you get down on yourself?" I asked gently. "I told you back at the Crabapple. You're *talented*, Liam."

"Yeah. Well. Someone described one of my recent shoots as 'the photographic equivalent of stick figures' and told me I shouldn't risk my current job to work on the book."

"Jealous asshat."

"Nah. This was a friend." He shook his head. "Someone who's generally pretty supportive."

"Your *friend* said your work was like stick figures? What do your enemies say?"

He snorted.

"Anyway, just 'cause they have an opinion doesn't mean they're right. Opinions are like assholes, right? Didn't your personal motto used to be '*The greater the risk, the greater the reward*'?"

He laughed. "Yeah. Sounds like some bullshit I'd've said. Hey, do you have a bowl for these veggies? I've basically pureed the peppers."

I got him a bowl and tried to hide my frown. Two minutes ago, I'd told him I wanted to keep things light because I couldn't handle hearing his reasons for leaving me. Now, the second the guy looked sad and mopey, I wanted to know every fucking detail of his life and demand the name and address of this shit-talking friend of his so I could kick their ass.

That was the moment when I began to think I was screwed where Liam McKnight was concerned. And not in the *fa la la-ing* fun way.

"You know, you could always—" I began.

"Actually." Liam held up a hand. "I think maybe you had a point about sticking to pie flavors tonight. Mine's chocolate, FYI. Chocolate brownie pie with thick, fresh cream."

I went along with the subject change.

"Is that a real *thing?*" I demanded.

He nodded, smacking his lips. "It's *so* a thing. Best thing you've ever put in your mouth, guaranteed."

"Hmmm. Bold statement. You have no idea what's been in my mouth."

"*God!*" Liam threw a tiny piece of pepper at me, and his eyes danced. "I'm having a perfectly innocent conversation about *pie*, and you had to take it there?"

"Me? *I* took it there? You're the one making an orgasm-face while talking about thick fresh cream. You *already* took us there."

I picked another pepper out of the bowl and tossed it at him. It landed on his cheek, but Liam was laughing too hard to notice.

"Hey." I reached out a hand slowly, like he was Fia and I was a stranger, and Liam froze, his eyes pinging from my face to my hand. I brushed my thumb over his cheekbone, wiping it clean…

And that's when I should have moved my hand away, right? Gone back to my side of the island? So I wasn't sure how to explain the way my palm cupped his face and my fingertips trailed back and forth across the light stubble at the hinge of his jaw, except to say that flames weren't *just* dangerous. They were beautiful and mysterious and warm and alluring too.

And I couldn't explain why Liam's cheek flushed hot beneath my hand, or why his gorgeous, *gorgeous* eyes went wide and glassy, or why his breathing hitched, except that maybe I was a fire in the night for him also, and he couldn't turn away any better than I could.

Hazel came skipping into the kitchen and then stopped short. "Daddy?"

Liam cleared his throat and took a step back. My hand dropped back to my side.

"Yeah, Bug! I, um, got some pepper on my face, and Gideon was helping me… clean it."

"Oh. Cool. Hey, Gideon?" She handed me a picture. "I noticed you don't have a lot of artwork around, so I made you some. It's Santa," she explained, like I might not have understood what the large red blob was.

But I understood only too well.

Santa Claus was fucking stalking me.

"It's… great. Very lifelike."

"I'll hang it on your refrigerator for you," she said helpfully, taking the picture from my hand and pinning it front and center on the fridge. "This way he can keep an eye on you."

I resisted the urge to shudder.

Liam's phone sounded, and he pulled it from his pocket. He looked at the screen, rolled his eyes, and set it down on the counter.

"Important?" I asked.

He shook his head. "Just that friend I mentioned,

commenting on something of mine that was in a local paper. No big deal."

"*Scott?*" Hazel demanded, and it was clear by her tone that whoever Scott was, he was persona non grata with the ten-and-unders.

"Hazel," Liam sighed. "Is it too late for me to start a *children should be seen and not heard* rule? Because I'm beginning to understand the appeal."

"Way too late," Hazel said matter-of-factly.

"Who's Scott?"

"He's Daddy's *friend*. They go out for *coffee*." She rolled her eyes. "He *fixes* Daddy's *collar*. And gives him *advice*."

"He *is* a friend," Liam insisted, but he blushed hotly. "A nice guy."

But Hazel's tone indicated that wasn't all he was, and I found myself clenching the spoon in my hand so hard my palm hurt.

Liam in, common sense out. As always.

I'd wondered why Liam had picked *now* to finally, officially divorce me, and I guess I had my answer.

Liam had moved on. And to a *nice guy*.

Pretty sure no one had ever accused me of being one of those.

It wasn't a huge surprise that he'd moved on. The surprising thing was that *I cared*. Apparently, I wasn't as over it—over *us*—as I'd assured Liam I was. Maybe a banged-up heart was a lot like a bump on the head, and there was internal damage even if it looked like everything was fine.

So that night, after I'd cleaned up the kitchen, after Liam and I had said a stilted goodnight, after the pint-sized con artist had carried my cat off to "her room" for a "sleepover party," and I was lying in my bed alone, I stared at the dresser across the room and felt the ring inside it pulsing like the telltale heart in that horror story we read in high school.

I thought about Liam's eyes and Hazel's smile.

I thought about how the world was a cold, cold place, and how I'd taught myself to be even *colder*... except when Liam was around.

I thought about how I was Ebenezer Scrooge, the crankiest person in O'Leary, and how I'd been visited by a ghost from my past so I could change things for my future.

I cursed Parker's interfering ass for making me even *consider* shit like this when I should have been sleeping soundly.

Then I threw off my covers and got out of bed.

Chapter Six

LIAM

"GIDEON HAS A SHOWER HEAD THAT MAKES IT *RAIN*," Hazel had informed me before climbing into bed, still shower-damp and bright-eyed despite it being *way* past her bedtime.

According to her, Gideon also had a nice voice. And the kindest smile. And the most amazing house. And the best cat *in the universe, Daddy*.

I'd nodded and smiled and pretended to agree because apparently teaching your children to be gracious guests was good parenting or something, but personally, I was thinking she was wrong.

Gideon's voice wasn't nice, it was sexy as fuck.

And his smile was sexy as fuck.

And those golden-brown eyes were sexy as fuck.

And his house was sexy as fuck, in the sense that his bedroom was three doors down the damn hall from my bedroom, and I could imagine him fucking me sexily in all his damn spare bedrooms.

But since none of that sexy fucking was gonna be happening, now or *ever again*, I figured I might as well use the rain shower to take care of some basic needs, you know? Needs like *cleanliness.* And *relaxation.*

Too bad I hadn't gotten much further than closing my eyes and wrapping my hand around my dick before the fucking weirdness of the situation assaulted me. I was jacking off thinking about *my husband* the night before I *divorced him.*

I wasn't sure what the Gracious Guest Handbook had to say about that, but I imagined it was nothing good.

I could say for sure it was a boner-killer.

I ruffled my hair with my fingers, scattering droplets around the little shower, and wrapped a towel that smelled like Gideon around my waist to make my way across the hall. If the sheets smelled like the towels, I might possibly be awake all—

"Jesus *fucking* Christ!" I exclaimed as Gideon's large form nearly ran me down as I stepped out of the bathroom.

"Oh." He seemed as surprised to see me as I was to see him. He grabbed both my biceps to steady me, then let go and took a step backward just as quickly. "I... I wanted to know... *do you need a blanket?*" His words were aggressive, like he was *daring* me to be chilly.

"I... No. I'm fine."

Gideon swallowed, his brown eyes tracking over the wet hair on my forehead. "I just... I was thinking... I want to talk."

"Talk? Now?" I blinked. "Uh. Okay?" I lifted a hand toward my door across the hall. "Go ahead."

He nodded once and stalked into the room. He got to the foot of the large, cherry sleigh bed, turned around to stare at my chest, and swallowed again.

"Look, I... I fucking hate talking."

I shook my head in confusion. "So, then—"

"I made a choice, a minute ago. I don't want to be angry anymore. And I thought you should know."

"Angry? Angry at *me*?"

"No." He ran a hand through his hair. "Maybe. Or more like, at *me*. Maybe it would be good to figure out what I did or failed to do that made you leave. And apologize. And then we can both… move on. Or something. Closure is a thing, isn't it?"

"Sure, but… You? Apologize?" I stared at him, my jaw hanging open like an idiot, but I couldn't help it because all thought had fled my brain. It had never, not once, occurred to me that Gideon might feel like *he* was at fault, that he'd think he'd ever been anything but… absolutely perfect.

"I do know how to apologize," he said hotly, then he paused. "In theory."

"Jesus, Gideon! You don't *need* to apologize. That's what I'm saying. It wasn't you *at all*. It was me. I just…" I rubbed my forehead. "I didn't have the luxury of doing what I wanted. I had Hazel to think about, and you and me… after I left, it felt like it couldn't have been real, you know?"

"Yeah." Gideon exhaled slowly. He was staring at my chest again. "I get that. I don't think about that time if I can help it, but when I do remember shit, I can't remember what's true and what I wanted to be true."

I nodded. I knew that feeling exactly.

"I have this one memory, or maybe I imagined it. You were on your knees for me," he whispered, and my heart thudded uncomfortably. "We were in the shower, and when you stared up at me, your eyelashes clumped together like stars. I touched your cheek, and I… I thought you were the most beautiful thing I'd ever seen, only I can't remember if I said it out loud."

Oh, sweet Jesus. This hurt.

"You did," I admitted softly. "And I said that I'd never been as happy as I was right then, and—"

"And if you could choose the last thought that flashed across your brain before you died it would be that day." His mouth twisted in a wry smile.

"Hey!" I bit my lip. "That was some deep shit right there, okay? Closest I'll ever get to writing poetry."

Gideon's eyes crinkled at the corners as we laughed at how sappy we'd been, but... looking at him in that moment, I realized that whatever else had changed in the last five years, that sentiment hadn't. I'd had happy moments with my daughter—a fuckton of them. But the happiest moment for *me?* The moments when I'd been most *Liam?* The most pure, unadulterated joy I could ever recall? Was the handful of hours I'd spent with him.

And maybe some part of that showed on my face because Gideon reached out a hand as far as he could toward me, and the very tip of his finger traced a rivulet of water down my chest.

I shivered at his touch. My nipples hardened. And beneath the towel, my cock—which hadn't seen any action in fucking *ages*—sprang to life like it had been waiting years for this opportunity.

Probably because it *had*.

He snatched his hand back and watched me warily.

And then it was like Vegas all over again.

I didn't know which of us moved first—maybe I reached for him, or he reached for me—but either way, it was clear that our talking time was done. Or maybe we were just finally communicating in a way that ensured no misunderstandings.

Gideon's strong arms wrapped around me, dragging my chest against his, and my entire body was wracked with chills suddenly, like I hadn't realized how cold I'd been until I was tucked in his warmth. Then his mouth found mine.

Holy shit.

He tasted so fucking good—like peppermint toothpaste and salt, totally wholesome and unreasonably sexy at once —and I pulled at the hem of his soft, gray t-shirt, eager to get to as much of his skin as I possibly could. He bent at the waist to help me and threw the shirt on the floor.

"*Fuck,*" he murmured when our chests brushed for the first time in five years. "*Fuck, fuck, fuck.* This is not what I'd expected when I came in here tonight."

He was hairy where I was smooth, tan where I was pale, and his broad chest and narrow waist were corded with lean muscle that made me lightheaded with the desire to taste him, but when his hands coasted down my arms to my wrists, he tangled our fingers together as his tongue stroked against mine, and then *Gideon* was the one who took a step back and dropped to his knees in front of me.

"Gideon," I whispered, and I wasn't sure if I meant to stop him or encourage him, or just say his name like a kind of magical incantation, but the next thing I knew, he'd pulled the towel off my waist, licked a path up my hard cock, and sucked me down.

Mother of God.

It had been a long time for me, yes. And a blow job was a blow job, true. But there was something about the sight of *this* big man kneeling on the beige carpet in his guest room, his lips spread wide around my cock, cheeks hollowed as he sucked me deep, that made me pretty fucking sure this was the best blowjob in history... at least in my personal history.

And it made my knees tremble.

I needed something to grab hold of, something concrete, and Gideon was all there was.

I ran my hand over his hair, over the short gray strands that looked spiky but were soft, and cradled his jaw, feeling his throat clench around me.

He looked up at me, his eyes dark with lust, and I was pretty sure I got what he was doing. He was inverting the memory of us five years ago.

"*Fuck.*" I pulled at his short hair, suddenly way too close to coming, and he seemed to get that. He pulled off with a *slurp* that sounded both obscene and perfect, and he rested his forehead against my stomach.

His breath came in warm bursts against my hip.

"*You're* the most beautiful thing *I've* ever seen," I said softly.

I had no idea where the words came from, and my stomach clenched because that was the *last* thing I should have said, but there was no space here in this quiet room for all the complexities and equivocations of daylight.

For Gideon and me, the truth always came out at night.

Gideon turned his face up to mine, his eyes alight and a little bit yearning, and I ignored the way my poor abandoned cock throbbed. Instead, I traced Gideon's straight, dark eyebrows, and smoothed the tiny *V* that appeared between them.

"Beautiful," I whispered again.

He sucked in a breath and shut his eyes, like it was too much, and when he opened them again, all his tenderness seemed to have coalesced into hunger. He pushed his pajama pants down, licked his palm, and began stroking his own cock, but before I had a chance to admire the view —because I was ready to settle in and pop some popcorn for that fucking show—his mouth was back on my cock and he sucked it greedily.

For half a second I felt a pang because I liked tender Gideon, but I pushed that thought away. I needed to come more than I needed tenderness. I needed the heat more than I needed to remember.

It felt like he was having some kind of race to see which of us he could get off first—either way, he'd win, and either way, he'd lose—and the only sounds in the world were my gasping breaths and the *slick slick slick* that I realized with a shiver was him working his own cock.

When I came an embarrassingly short time later, my release spilled down his throat, and it was so fucking *good* that I doubled over, one hand on his head and the other on the wall behind him.

A thought flitted across my brain that there was a reason why no one had ever gotten to me the way Gideon did, neither before nor since, but my brain was way too busy trying to obtain oxygen to catch it.

Gideon stood up while I was still catching my breath, dislodging my hand from his hair as he tucked himself back into his pajama pants. At first, I wasn't sure whether he'd even come, but then I saw the wet spot that had conveniently landed on his discarded shirt.

"Wow," I said. "That was… a hell of a talk."

It was meant as a joke. *Haha.* A kind of *holy shit, I just had sex with my husband, what does this mean?* icebreaker… not that, you know, anyone else in the universe felt this level of unease about sleeping with their spouse.

But Gideon looked at me and nodded once, like I'd confirmed something I totally had *not* meant to confirm. He gave me a lopsided smile and reached out a finger to brush my cheek. "You have a good night, Liam. I'll see you in the morning."

And then he walked out the door and left me shivering and cold.

Chapter Seven

LIAM

GIDEON PULLED HIS TRUCK INTO A SPOT A FEW DOORS down from the bakery Friday morning with a giant smile on his face, and I resisted the urge to scowl in response.

The phone in my pocket had pinged with a text as soon as I'd put the Volvo in park a minute ago, but I hadn't checked it. It could have been my mother, still awake in California and sending me some article about how children needed to listen to organic tantric goat sounds, but also telling me she wouldn't be coming for Christmas. It could possibly have been my editor checking to see whether I really needed three *full* days off, like that was the kind of thing a person joked about. Either way, not something I felt equipped to deal with that morning. My car was low on gas, my body was low on caffeine, and I was very, *very* low on patience.

Hazel ran over to Gideon's truck the second he'd parked and started chattering to him in a light, happy voice, like they'd been separated for years instead of mere minutes, and he rumbled something in response.

They seemed to be in a *fine* mood. Gideon seemed lit-up

from the inside out, his golden-brown eyes shining like he'd had a delightful orgasm the night before followed by eight solid hours of rest, and tiny fucking fairies had come to wake him from slumber, sprinkling him with just a little *extra* sexy-dust today. Meanwhile, Hazel hadn't stopped talking about how she was going to eat "*a mountain of frosting, oh my gosh!*" and reminding me that she'd spent the night cuddling with an "*actual, real, live cat, Daddy!*"

I rolled my eyes. It didn't take a psychic to predict the hot topic on the ride home, and I was planning to launch an offensive Kiddie Bop attack before we'd even reached the O'Leary border. Painful as that might be, at least with Kiddie Bop I wouldn't be scooping kitty litter for the rest of my natural life.

Bah fucking humbug.

I slid my phone from my pocket finally and frowned down at the screen.

Scott: Morning, sunshine. Will you be home in time to meet for drinks tonight?

I frowned harder. Was he kidding?

There were three things wrong with this text.

One, since when did Scott and I meet for drinks? Maybe I'd binged too much *Sex and the City* with Livia back in the day, but coffee consumed during the day near your office was one thing, and meeting for drinks on a Friday evening, outside my normally scheduled babysitter times, was something else entirely. If I'd had a Carrie or a Samantha in my life, I'd have called to discuss, but the closest I had was my sister, and I was too tired to do the math on what time it was in Ulaanbaatar.

Second, and continuing in the same vein, since when the fuck was I "sunshine"? Was I reading too much meaning into a single word in a single text? Or had I not been reading enough meaning into all the words in all the texts up to now? Or did it only matter because I'd had my dick in Gideon's mouth a matter of hours ago, and the idea of being Scott's *sunshine* felt extra-specially wrong?

Third, while it was technically morning, I personally ascribed to the belief that if you hadn't closed your eyes the night before, it was still one very long, very bright night, and Scott's perkiness offended me on a deep, personal level.

"Daddy! Hurry *up!*" Hazel called from halfway down the block, where she was walking with her little hand in Gideon's larger one, their arms swinging in a way that would have been adorable if it wasn't *freaking me out*.

Then again, everything was low-key freaking me out. First and foremost: the way I could still feel the heat of Gideon's body pressed against mine, despite the chill in the air. See also: the way I'd tossed and turned all night, pissed at myself for falling back into something with Gideon, even though it was no more responsible now than it had been five years ago, and probably even less so.

What if he got the wrong idea and thought us being... *intimate...* meant we were back to being *together?* What if he decided to contest the divorce, or fuck around with finances, or bring up *Hazel?*

And no, okay, if I was being real, I didn't think there was any way in the world that Gideon was going to make Hazel's life difficult even if he *did* get the wrong idea, but... the whole point of being a parent was that you didn't take chances with shit like that.

And yet, here I was.

I blew out a breath and slid my phone back into my pocket without replying. Scott could wait until I'd had enough coffee to make sense of my life.

Gideon held the door open for me and winked when I passed him, which hit my stomach like a bolt of adrenaline, the same way the scents of vanilla and butter and cinnamon hit me as soon as I stepped inside.

The bakery was *mobbed*—Cal, Ash, and a curly-haired woman I hadn't met the day before were working behind the counter with a coordination that almost seemed choreographed, and at least twenty people stood in line, all talking, chatting, and laughing amongst themselves. But nobody was pushing, tapping their foot impatiently, staring at their phone, or huffing. In fact, there were *maybe* two people on cell phones in the whole place, whereas at least a dozen people were wearing Santa hats, and what kind of Narnia was this where the ratio of cell phones to Santa hats was that low?

Even more miraculously, Cal spotted the three of us standing by the door, stopped what he was doing, and *waved*.

"Liam! Gideon! *Hazel!* Have a seat!" He pointed to the one empty table in the place.

"Don't we have to order?" I whispered to Gideon. "And, like, *pay?*"

Gideon smirked. "Apparently not when you're with a VIP." He nodded at Hazel, who'd already taken a seat.

Our table was short a chair, but in the same instant I noticed it, someone stood up from the next table over and moved their chair next to Hazel.

"Thanks, Micah," Gideon said with a chin lift.

"Sure. Welcome to O'Leary, Liam," Micah said to me.

"Um. Thanks." What was with this town being so overly friendly? What was with them *knowing who I was?* "You sure you're not using it?" I asked, nodding at the chair.

"Yep, positive. I'm already late opening the shop. Constantine's been *distracting*." He jerked a thumb over his shoulder at the guy sitting behind him.

"Hey!" His companion—a guy whose blue eyes reminded me a little of Julian from the night before—glanced up, and the two exchanged a look so hot I nearly gasped. "Do I hear complaining?"

"Nope. But your tardiness will be noted in your annual review. You'll have to work extra hard if you want that raise."

Constantine gave him a smile that managed to be angelic and filthy at the same time. "I appreciate the opportunity, *boss*."

Micah braced his hand on the back of Constantine's chair and leaned down to kiss him, Constantine's hand came up so his fingers could grab at Micah's shirt just above his waist in this desperate little *clutch-release-clutch-release* move that was hotter than many a cumshot I'd watched over the years, and when Micah leaned back five seconds later, Constantine looked at him with this expression that just… *gah*.

Extremely similar to the look Gideon had given me last night.

The whole thing was PG or PG-13 at most, but I felt like I needed a shower. And honestly, was that really *appropriate*? Did a person really need to be *visually assaulted* with a bird's eye view of everything he wanted and would never, ever have *before he'd eaten breakfast*?

"Sit," Gideon directed, holding out a chair for me with a vaguely amused expression. "Before you attack someone. What's got you worked up?"

I huffed out a breath and dropped into the chair.

"Sorry. *Sorry*. Just, like… have you ever felt like the whole world was full of fu—*fa la la-ing* sunshine and fairies, and you just wanted to be left alone to be a human pillar of salt?"

"Who, me?" Gideon's lips twitched, but he shook his head solemnly. "Never."

"Never, huh?"

"I'm a perpetual ray of sunshine, Liam. Especially around the holidays."

I snorted and shrugged out of my jacket, noticing that Gideon had already helped Hazel out of hers. "Sorry," I said again. "Not sure what my problem is today."

Except I was pretty sure I *did*. And it was sitting next to me, watching me with tawny eyes.

"I'd sort of imagined you'd be… *relaxed* today. Did you sleep alright?" Gideon asked, a tiny pucker between his brows. "Bed uncomfortable?"

Yes. The sheets smelled uncomfortably just like you and I was uncomfortably aware that I'd just come down my soon-to-be-ex-husband's throat and I felt uncomfortably similar to the way I'd felt five years ago.

"Nah," I said. "It was great."

"Hey!" Cal appeared next to our table with a tray in his hands. "So, kind of a good news, bad news situation for you."

Gideon lifted an eyebrow. "What's the bad news?"

"Wellll, Paul Fine's sick with the stomach flu. So… still no notary in town."

I folded my arms over my chest. "Really. This wouldn't be a ploy to get us to stay an extra night?"

Cal winced. "You, ah… you cottoned on to that?"

"Just a little," I confirmed.

"You're saying I won't be nominated for an Oscar?"

"'Fraid not," Gideon said.

"Ah, well. Anyway, I'm serious about the flu. Quinn, that's Paul's husband," he added with a nod to me, "was in earlier to get some coffee because he can't brew it in the house without… you know." He made a retching noise.

"Charming," Gideon said.

I rubbed my forehead. "What's the good news?"

"Well." Cal set the tray in the center of the tiny table. "Mountains of frosting today, pumpkin cream cheese muffins tomorrow?"

"Yes!" Hazel said, quietly exultant. "What's on Sunday?"

Gideon and I exchanged a look, and I expected an explosion of outrage. I expected him to turn the air blue with his *fa la las*.

Instead, to my shock, he gave a resigned sigh. "Sucks, but what can you do?"

I stared at him, wondering if he'd *literally* orgasmed his brain out the night before, or if he was always this slow in the morning.

"Uh, we can find someone else." *Duh.* "If we don't get this done today, that means me sticking around until *Monday*!"

"Yeah, I figured." Gideon nodded. "It's fine—"

I shook my head vehemently. "It's *so* not. What's the closest town? Rushton? I'm guessing they have a notary, right? I mean, we're not looking for a fu—" I took a deep breath. "A *fa la la-ing* unicorn here, Gideon!" I fought to keep my voice calm and failed.

Fortunately, Hazel was too frosting-delirious to notice.

"They do!" Cal looked sympathetic and maybe a trifle wary. "But Rushton has a festival very similar to our winter festival—"

Constantine leaned toward our table and said darkly, "Lies. It's a pitiful imitation."

"I don't think Liam cares, Connie. Thing is, that's tomorrow—"

"Because they think if they have it a week before ours,

they can take bragging rights!" Henry called from a table by the window.

"What Cal's trying to say is that Rushton's more or less closed down today and tomorrow for the preparation and the festival. Kids are off school and businesses are closed." Gideon shrugged. "It's a thing."

"It's a *fa la la-ing* insane *thing*!" I said desperately.

"Wouldn't it be awesome to go to school here?" Hazel asked no one in particular. Her mouth was brown with cinnamon, and her teeth were gooey with frosting.

"'Fraid it's not always like that, Hazel Grace," Gideon informed her. "Kids here get fewer snow days than other places. It all evens out."

She shrugged, unconcerned about theoretical snow days when she could have a very real day off *now*, and I very much envied that ability to live in the moment.

"What about the town I passed on the way here?" I looked around the bakery. "Camden?"

Caelan looked at Gideon, who shrugged and looked at Con, who shrugged and pulled out his phone.

"According to the internet, Phil Grant is the only result," he said gloomily.

"Oh, no way. No. *Nope*!" Ash called from behind the counter. "Cal, you remember him? From when we were sorting out our legal stuff?"

"I remember," Cal said. "Phil Grant is a homophobic piece of… *candy*." He glanced at Hazel. "The nastiest, most vile… candy. I'm sure he'd love to help you two get your—"

"*Grown-up business*!" I interrupted, tilting my head toward Hazel significantly.

"Right. He'd love to help you with that, and he'd be smirking the whole time. Seriously, he's awful."

I rubbed my face with two hands, exhausted and frustrated.

"But Rick might be back any day now," Cal soothed. "Ross is doing better. And if the weather gets warmer, Jay Turner might be able to—"

"I have a *job*," I said from behind my hands. "Hazel has *school*. We can't just stay here and hang out indefinitely! There has *got* to be a notary between here and *Boston*." I dropped my hands and shot Gideon a pleading look. "I know it's a pain, but can't we drive a little farther—"

Gideon's lips pinched. "I have a shift at the station at one, and there's no one to cover me." His voice was soft and apologetic. "But I get two days in a row off next week, if it comes to that—"

I closed my eyes and nodded, breathing in the smell of coffee and vanilla. What were the chances that I was gonna be able to stay at Gideon's for two more nights without being tempted to be with him again?

But whatever. *Okay*. This was *fine*. This was… *doable*. I'd be tempted, but I didn't have to *act* on it. I could lock my door. I could bunk with Hazel. Something.

I clenched my teeth. And opened my eyes. To find that my daughter hadn't so much consumed a cinnamon roll as been consumed *by* one.

At least one of us was sure to be okay with this change of plans. And honestly, of the two of us, her happiness was the most important, right?

I shook my head wryly, grabbed a napkin from the little dispenser on the side of the table, and motioned Hazel to lean closer so I could wipe her mouth.

"Hey, um, Liam?" Constantine leaned over toward our table. "I was delivering flowers at the Crabapple first-first thing this morning, and *Dana* said *you* said you were a photographer?"

"Oh." I frowned. "Yeah."

"And *she* said *Gideon* said you were super talented."

I blinked. "I…"

"So, like, could you take a picture of me and Micah? Something I could make into a big *thing* for the wall? I'd gladly pay you, and that might make up some of the income you'd be losing, having to stick around."

"Well. I mean, I guess—"

"Oh, wait!" Ash exclaimed. "I need to be in on this action. Cal, you and me, ugly sweaters and Santa hats, and we send out cheesy cards to everyone—"

Cal was already shaking his head. "There is no universe, Ashley Martin, where I am going to be captured for posterity wearing an ugly sweater."

"But the hats are a go?" Ash wiggled his eyebrows.

"Also no." He gave me a crooked smile. "But Ash is right. We'd love to get professional photos. We have, ah, wedding stuff to send out soon."

A chair pushed back with a loud scrape, and a blonde woman stood and peered over Hazel's head at me.

"*A professional* photographer? Whose pictures have you done?"

"He didn't bring a resume, Karen." Cal folded his arms over his chest.

"But his work's been in magazines," Con added. "Dana said so."

The Karen person sniffed. "I've been *dying* to get pictures of my baby Brantley. I'm thinking something with angel wings? Possibly laying on a cloud of rose petals? But no one around here is competent, and you have *no idea* how difficult it is to drive long distances with an infant."

"You're right," I agreed. "I don't." I wasn't sure whether to inform her that driving with slightly older children was no picnic either.

Gideon looked at me sharply.

"What?"

His expression blanked. "No, nothing. Just... thinking. Okay, who's got paper and pen for an appointment sign-up sheet?" He looked expectantly at Cal and Ash.

"On it," Ash said, heading into the backroom.

I shook my head. "But I... I don't have a space. I don't have lights. I don't have a backdrop..."

"I've got backdrops if you need them," a dark-haired man sitting with Henry volunteered. "And Grandpa's probably got whatever kind of lights you need."

Henry nodded. "A good thought, Everett. You know, Diane and I could get a picture done. Maybe with Daphne."

"A family portrait of you, your girlfriend, and *my* cat?" Everett rolled his eyes. "This makes not one iota of sense, and yet I'm not remotely surprised."

"You're just jealous your cat likes me better than you," Henry said with a sniff. "Don't worry. Pretty sure Silas still likes you best... for now."

Everett snorted.

"And there's lots of places outdoors you could take pictures if you want—up at the campground by the waterfall or over at the fairgrounds with the gazebo. Be real pretty with some holiday lights!" a woman I'd never seen before volunteered.

"And what about the empty office over Hardison's for indoor stuff?" The man sitting with her suggested. "You could talk to Jen Hardison, but I don't think they're gonna be doing anything with it this month. Betcha they'd let you use it for free."

"I can watch Hazel for you," Sam, the teenager from yesterday said, waving her hand. She grinned at my daughter. "Discounted rates. We could have *so* much fun. We could go to the library, we can make cookies, we can do crafts."

Hazel's eyes widened, then narrowed, searching for the catch. "How do you feel about *Beyoncé*?"

Sam gave an exaggerated eye roll. "*Is* there more than one way to feel about Queen Bee?"

"I like this plan, Daddy," Hazel informed me seriously. "A *lot*."

I bit my lip. A dozen friendly faces were turned in my direction, all waiting for me to say, "*Yes!*" And I wanted to. I did. But also… who the hell *were* these people, and what were they going to expect from me in return?

When my phone rang in my pocket, I jumped up immediately and grabbed my coat, eager for an excuse to get away. "I need to get this," I said, without looking at the screen. "Be right back."

I pushed my way outside into the cold, clean air and took a deep breath, then accepted the call.

"Scott. Hey."

"Don't *hey* me!" Scott's voice, sarcastic and familiar, was like a shock of vinegar after a sickly-sweet morning. "Three texts, no reply, I was starting to take it personally."

In addition to the text this morning, Scott had sent a couple of texts last night. The first, a critique of a photo of mine, had arrived while we were cooking dinner. The second, a follow-up asking if I was upset, came while I was still so orgasm-drunk I couldn't feel my toes.

"It's been a day and a half, and I told you I was going out of town," I reminded him. "I've been busy."

"Uh huh." His voice was knowing, like he'd caught me out. "You know, you really need to develop a thicker skin, Liam. I don't know how you think you're ready to publish a book when you can't handle even the most minor feedback."

Considering I hadn't asked for a critique, and since the picture was already *printed*, the criticism went beyond unhelpful into downright rude, and Gideon's "jealous asshat" comment from the night before stuck with me. I'd never really thought about the dynamic of my friendship with Scott before, and now I couldn't help it.

Not that I thought Scott was *jealous* of me—he wasn't. Just that his way of giving advice didn't inspire me to be better at what I was doing. And it was kinda fucked up that Gideon, who had every reason to be mad at me for leaving five years ago and crashing back into his life right now, was all, "Keep going, Liam! Trust your talent! *Rah rah!*" in a way that made me feel *capable*, whereas Scott, who was my easy, uncomplicated friend, sometimes made me feel worse.

Or, maybe I was really just thin-skinned, like Scott said, and accepting Gideon's praise felt nice.

I ignored his comments and focused on keeping things light. "I've been genuinely busy last night *and* this morning. Remember, I have a daughter who enjoys being fed with regularity?"

"Oh, I remember. Hazel's the reason I haven't been able to take you out to *Orelline*," he teased. "Remember, I was telling you about the orzo with fennel pollen?"

I remembered not knowing fennel pollen was edible.

"*She's* not the reason, Scott," I said stiffly. "I am. Being her parent is my highest priority, and I'm not sure I'm ready—"

"No, no, I know," he said dismissively. "But you will be. Sometime soon we'll go."

I sighed. "Not that soon. We're going to be in O'Leary longer than I thought. I have business to take care of."

"What kind of business? And what's O'Leary?"

"A town in Upstate New York. Tiniest town in the

world." I glanced through the bakery window and saw over a dozen townspeople clustered loosely around the table where Gideon and Hazel still sat, figuring out my life for me. "Possibly fictional."

"*What?*"

"Nothing. It's just a really nice place. You'd have to see it sometime to really believe it. Really…" I looked up Weaver Street, where colored lights and greenery adorned every shop, and a guy dressed as Santa handed out flyers in front of the bed and breakfast. "Really picturesque. Really friendly. I've had people offering me jobs and discounted babysitting, even though I'm a perfect stranger." I snorted. "Can you imagine that in Boston?"

"Uh, no. For a *reason*." Scott's tone hit somewhere between dismay and disgust. "Liam, you *have* a job. And you're not going to let just anyone watch Hazel, are you? Someone you've never met before now and haven't fully vetted?"

"I—"

"Seriously, Liam, what are you thinking? Is everything okay? Do you need my help? I know you *hate* taking help from anyone—"

"Not true!" I said, stung. "I take help!" But no one offered the help I *needed*.

The bell on the bakery door chimed, and Gideon stepped outside. He looked me up and down, then frowned.

"Everything okay?" he asked softly.

Define okay. Because this thing with Scott is not okay, and the way I feel lightning-struck every time I'm around you is not okay, and staying with you means wanting you because I can't not *and that is not okay…*

I nodded.

"I've, um… I've gotta go," I said into the phone as Gideon took a step toward me.

"Wait, no! When will you be back? We can reschedule that drink—"

"A few more days. I'll let you know." I hung up without regret.

"So," I said to the man standing in front of me. His eyes tracked my features like he was trying to see inside my head. "What's up?"

"Came out here to ask you that." He lifted his hand to my ear—the one that hadn't had the phone pressed to it—and I shivered at the heat of his hand against my cold skin. "Don't you have a hat?"

I shook my head and resisted the urge to lean toward him. Gideon made a good wind break. "This was supposed to be a two-day thing, remember? With most of that time spent in the car?"

The hand on my ear moved to the back of my neck, rubbing lightly. "How upset are you about this delay, *really*?"

"*Really*?" I huffed out a breath. "I'm pretty fucking upset! We're gonna have to stay with you—"

"I don't mind."

"Yeah?" I tilted my head. "Because last night, you wanted to pawn us off on anyone with a spare room, and then you and I—" I broke off and ran a hand through my hair. "Then last night happened, and now you're all 'no, it's fine,' and I just… I don't think that's a good idea, you know? I don't think…"

"Liam, what did I say to you last night?" Gideon's voice was low and hypnotic, and his fingers prodded my neck with just the right pressure.

I licked my lips. "Um. Which part? You said… a lot of things."

"The part where I said I wasn't gonna be angry anymore. You remember that?"

I sighed. "But then you... and we... and I just..."

His second hand came up to join the first, splaying into my hair, tugging gently against my scalp. I let out a pitiful moan.

"Yesterday, I was tired after a long shift. I got the shock of my life seeing you. Seeing *Hazel.* Dealing with that bunch of shit stirrers." He nodded over my head into the bakery. "But it was nice having you both there. And, not gonna lie, it was *really* nice not having Fia walking on my head at five a.m., waiting to be fed."

"But—"

"I have no expectations, Liam. Sex is off the table unless you say different, okay?"

I frowned up at him. I wasn't trying to be argumentative; I just couldn't help feeling like I was missing something. Like my brain was foggy.

"But then why would you—" I shook my head. "Why would you be so nice to me?"

"You think I'm nice? *Pfft.* Please. It's all part of my cunning, evil plan."

"Yeah? To do what?"

Gideon snorted. "I have no fucking idea." He shook his head once, like he was darkly amused, possibly at himself. "I just... can't... see you unhappy." He shrugged like it was no big deal, but a muscle ticked in his jaw. "It's one of those weird things. An instinctive reaction I can't turn off, even though I want to. If I *can* help you, I will."

I stared at him. No one in my life had ever said something like that to me, and I wasn't sure how to feel about it.

"Those people in there"— I pointed over my shoulder —"are trying to get us together and we... I... I can't let it happen again, Gideon."

"Then don't. You're not a kid, Liam, and no one is forcing your hand. I'm not, and I won't let anyone else either. You get me?"

I sighed. "You think I'm being stupid, don't you?"

"Stupid? Never. You're reacting very normally for a person who's never lived in the Narnia that is O'Leary, New York. But I've lived here a few years now. I know these folks are good people. They're *crazy*, and they'll tell you they've got snakes in their heating ducts because they wanna play matchmaker, but they're basically good folks. And while their motives were flat-out wacky in this case, the help they're offering is what they'd offer anyone in this town who needed it. So you can take it, or you can leave it. It's your choice. And either way, we'll make the best of it."

Gideon's breath was a sweet rush over my skin, and his fingers on my neck were magic.

"It's okay that you don't trust them. I get it," Gideon said. "But you *can* trust *me*, Liam. And I'm telling you, it's gonna be okay."

Damn, I wanted to believe that. I wanted to believe it so much, I stepped away.

"Hey, if this whole firefighting thing doesn't work out, massage school might be a good option for you. Thanks for that."

Gideon stared at the hand that had been touching me like he wasn't quite sure where it had come from. Then he closed it into a fist and stuck the fist into his pocket.

He cleared his throat. "You ready to come finish your breakfast?"

I forced a smile. "Yes. I think I might be ready to scale the mountains of frosting now." I stepped toward the door.

Gideon grabbed my elbow. He looked… hesitant. Like he was struggling with how to say something. "Look, if you really need to get home, I'm sure there's some way I can get my part done, and you can get your part done yourself. Or I could see if I could take a day off sooner than later. Or—"

I thought about it, a little bit overwhelmed that Gideon really *was* committed to giving me as many choices as possible, but I shook my head. "Not positive, but I'm pretty sure we need to sign the forms together. That's part of why I came instead of just mailing them. And I don't want to make you take time off." I sighed. "It can wait another day or two."

"It's been five years already, right?" He shot me a sardonic glance that made my stomach tighten with want and held out a hand to lead me back inside. "We can wait and tackle it together?"

I'd told myself a bunch of lies over the years—that Gideon's eyes hadn't been that golden, that his hands *hadn't* been that large and capable, that the connection I'd imagined had been lust or jet lag or temporary insanity, that he hadn't been that *kind*—and I'd nearly managed to convince myself that they were true.

But honestly? Gideon *was* that great. We *had* been that connected. And now we weren't. And while I stood behind my decision then and now… it really fucking sucked.

I hadn't just been in love with Gideon Mason, I *liked* him too.

I still did.

"Together," I agreed, taking his hand. Until we weren't anymore.

Chapter Eight

LIAM

"THAT GOOD?" EVERETT ASKED, STEPPING BACK FROM A tall spotlight he'd requisitioned from his grandfather's hardware store, and brushing his curly black hair out of his eyes.

Somehow, in less than forty minutes, the two of us had managed to push the old office furniture to either side of the brightly lit space, cover the slightly dingy walls and neutral industrial carpet with a wintery backdrop Everett had painted, and even set up folding chairs so that my "clients" could wait their turn.

It was the closest thing to a Christmas miracle I was likely to experience.

I looked through the lens of my camera at the backdrop and gave Ev a thumbs up. "I might need to adjust as I lose the natural light later, but I think that's as good as we're gonna get for right now?" I shot him a grateful glance. "Thanks so much for taking the time off school to help me with this, leaving all those young minds without an art teacher."

Everett chuckled. "Fridays are light for me. I don't have to teach another class until noon. And besides, photography's always fascinated me."

I nodded and toed at a box of decorative props—a jumble of giant plush candy canes, wooden gingerbread men, and enormous gilt stars—that some woman I'd never met had dropped off with a friendly wink. "You paint, right?"

"Yeah! I mean… if you look at the pieces I've produced this past year, you'd think O'Leary festival paraphernalia was my area of expertise." He rolled his eyes and nodded at the blue-and-silver snow-covered backdrop. "Not my preferred medium, but I'm getting used to it."

"You've had to paint more than one backdrop?" I remembered Gideon saying there were too many festivals in town, but…"How many backdrop-requiring events are there?"

"Oh, something like… eighteen?"

My shock must've shown on my face because Everett laughed. "I know, right? I used to think it was weird too, when I first moved here. But I've, ah… drunk the Kool-Aid." He smiled a smile I couldn't decipher.

"You're an O'Leary transplant?"

He nodded. "From Boston, like you. My mom was born and raised here, but she left as soon as she was legal, and I only moved here and started teaching, mmm… God, sixteen months ago now?" Ev shook his head. "It seems both longer and shorter."

"Did you find it *weird*?" I demanded.

"Shit, yeah. Still do sometimes. It's the most bizarre culture shock imaginable. Out *there* they have Uber and dim sum and neighbors who understand boundaries, whereas here in O'Leary you have to walk to the bakery and every single person in town knows *exactly* what you ordered."

"Right? That's exactly it! In Boston, I have a life where it's just me and Hazel, and one nice neighbor who babysits because I pay her, you know? Suddenly, I'm here for twenty-four hours and my child is off with someone I barely know, and all one-thousand-seventy-something people in town have donated stuff to help me out." I toed the box again and felt compelled to admit, "You know, I told Gideon nothing is gonna happen between us. It can't."

Everett frowned. "Okay. What's one thing gotta do with the other?"

I shrugged. "I don't know. Gideon said it had nothing to do with anything, but... I feel like you're all helping because you care about Gideon, and you wanna play matchmaker—like all that shit with the vipers and the hotel—and you're gonna be pissed when I end up leaving next week."

Everett nodded, like he'd heard all the stories, and he probably had. "I see. Yeah. Because out there, with the McDonald's and the boundaries, it's all quid pro quo. It's not like that here, Liam. There's a reason I've stayed in this town, you know?"

I frowned. "Yeah. Because you're with someone here, right? Silas?"

Ev smiled and leaned back against one of the ancient, melamine desks. "You sound like me when I first came here. 'What's the catch? What's the lowest common denominator?' Yeah, I'm with Silas. But he loves me, and if I wasn't happy here, he'd have moved." It was a simple statement of fact, and his eyes were warm. "We stayed because for all the insanity in O'Leary, it's a good place. A place you can count on."

"You sound like Gideon."

"Because he knows what he's talking about."

"People do seem nice," I allowed. "Generous."

Gideon certainly was.

Everett was silent for a second, then he crouched down to start sorting through the props in the box at my feet.

"Did you know there's a Santa contest in town, Liam?"

"No! But that explains a lot. There's an overabundance of Santa hats out there. I thought it was a weird kind of fashion."

Everett grinned. "Yeah, wait until next week when the full costumes get broken out." He shook his head indulgently. "Anyway, the thing is, the costumes aren't even the point of the contest. Like, it's not about who can *look* most like Santa. The idea is to basically *be* Santa. To do good deeds and expect nothing in return, *ho ho ho*."

"Seriously?" I asked. "That's so…" I couldn't figure out how to finish that. Silly? Sweet?

"The word you're looking for is '*O'Leary*,'" Everett said. "As in, 'That's so O'Leary.' And this place will drive you *batshit*, let me just tell you. People asking when you're gonna have kids, and commenting on how they love or hate your new sweater, and judging any new guy or gal you bring home, and checking out whether you're buying whole or skim milk at the Imperial." He shook his head. "It's like having a thousand loving, crazy-making relatives. But Liam, if you decide to leave, you leave. They might shake their heads and wish they'd done something even *crazier* to keep you here, but they're not gonna be mad or whatever."

"*When* I leave," I corrected.

"Sure," he agreed easily. "*When*."

He sorted props silently for a minute, then chucked a plastic snowflake back in the box impatiently. "Okay, fuck it. I've been sitting here trying to remember to mind my own business, but apparently it takes exactly sixteen months to be assimilated by the Borg because I've completely forgotten how to be normal." He brushed his hair out of his eyes again. "What *is* the deal with you and Gideon? You're *married*?"

I hesitated, but it was hardly a *secret*, right? And Jesus, I really needed someone to talk to.

I dropped to my ass on the carpet on the other side of the prop box and resumed Everett's sorting job.

"Gideon and I met five years ago this month at the Paris Hotel in Las Vegas."

"Vegas," Everett repeated. "Our Gideon?"

I laughed. "Yeah. He was in town for a college friend's bachelor party, and he picked me up at a hotel bar. Or I picked him up. It's a contested subject." I found myself smiling a bit, remembering Gideon and me debating it… in bed together.

"Okay, now I seriously need to know more."

"Well…" Normally I hated even thinking about this shit, let alone talking about it. I hated remembering Gideon's face or the time we'd spent together. I hated even mentioning his *name*. But now, sitting with someone who knew him, knowing I'd get to see him for two more nights, remembering came easily.

"Okay, so I was in Vegas for a weekend doing a photo-shoot of interesting sunrise and sunset landscapes." I shrugged. "They wanted backgrounds for an ad campaign for watches."

Everett nodded.

"I hardly ever got jet lagged, but that particular trip, I'd been up all night, and then I'd slept all day, so I was groggy even though it was six in the evening. And on top of *that* I was *dehydrated* because I'd been out in the desert. So I'm sitting at the bar, getting a drink and a snack, minding my own business, and just… suffice it to say, I was not *remotely* down to fuck, even if Idris Elba had walked into the bar and begged me, you know?" I paused, considering. "Okay, maybe if he'd begged."

He grinned. "Sure. Allowances must be made."

I nodded. "So anyway, this guy sits down on the stool next to me—like, *right* next to me, even though the place was half empty, getting all up in my personal space, and I'm thinking this is just *weird* because how the hell would he even know I was into guys, you know?"

"Right!"

"So I turned to go *off* on him for being a presumptuous asshole, and… *zing*."

"Zing?" Everett looked amused.

"Yeah. Just… I don't know what sound two magnets make when they align toward each other, but I imagine it sounds a lot like *zing*."

Everett's smile widened. "And then what?"

"We went up to my room. Worlds were rocked, lives were changed."

"Wow. When you were still half-asleep and dehydrated?"

"That's the thing," I said slowly. "I wasn't. From the moment I looked at him, I was wide awake. And I don't just mean physically. I just… I'd never been more… myself."

"Really." Everett sounded a little skeptical. "That fast?"

I shrugged. "You know how there's always a certain level of *effort* when you first hook up with a guy? You laugh at *all* the jokes, even the ones that aren't funny? And things feel nice, obviously, but like, ten percent of your brain isn't quite there because it's busy obsessing that your breath isn't fresh enough and you haven't spent enough time at the gym?"

"Highly relatable, yes."

I nodded once. "There was none of that with Gideon. Not a single minute of wondering what he was thinking or wondering if it was good for him. No thinking *period*. It was like I could read his mind, or maybe he could read mine, because he gave me all the words I needed before I even knew I needed them, and everything felt so—" I broke off, shaking my head.

"Zing?" Ev supplied.

"Yeah," I agreed. "Exactly."

"And?"

"And we got married. By Elvis. As one does." I shook my head. "I'm making it sound stupid, but at the time I… I loved him. I don't think… I mean, I didn't really consider in that moment if it was the kind of love that would last until the end of *time*, but… I didn't have much that was mine back then. My parents liked to think of themselves as nomads, and they raised me and my sister to be the same. I traveled light. I didn't have a lot of people or places I was attached to. But with him, it wasn't a choice, really."

"You just *were* attached."

"Yeah." I blew out a breath. "Anyway. I've got like thirty minutes until Micah and Con arrive, and you need to get back to the school, so…"

"No way!" Everett said. "No no no, you can't leave me hanging. *Then* what?"

"Then…" *Then* the phone rang in the drawn-curtain darkness of our bedroom, and I was alone and completely unprepared for the voice on the other end.

Then I was hopping around the room trying to find my clothes, suitcase, shoes, and wallet in the *dark* because adrenaline leaves no room for logical choices like opening the curtains or turning on a light.

Then I was on the way to the airport, flying toward the

biggest job of my *life*, and it wasn't until I was on the plane, an hour after the phone call, and I'd checked my passport, phone, and ticket for the twelfth time, that I realized why I had the nagging feeling I'd forgotten something vitally important: Gideon had no idea where I'd gone.

And I was such a fucking idiot, I'd gotten *married* to the man without knowing his cell phone number.

Which, you know, was the kind of horrifying realization I should have had *before* tying myself legally to a perfect stranger.

There was an order to these things *for a reason*.

"Then I realized I had responsibilities," I told Everett sadly because that's what it all boiled down to in the end, right? "And wanting to be with Gideon was the selfish choice, not the right choice. So I left."

"You… left. Just like that?"

I searched his face for anger or judgement, but he just seemed confused.

"Kinda, yeah. I thought about contacting him a million times, but… at first, it would have been too hard because I missed him, and I figured a clean break would be best." I shrugged. "After that, it would've been too hard because I had my life—my *kid*—to take care of, and I figured he'd moved on. What good would it have done to explain all this stuff?"

Ev winced, and I remembered Gideon saying, *"What could I have done better?"*

"It was shitty," I said baldly. "Just… poorly done. I don't regret leaving, but I regret the way I left."

"Have you told him that?"

I shook my head. "He doesn't want explanations. He claims he's not angry anymore. He claims he can't *not* be nice to me. But… how?" I ran a hand through my hair. "And *this* is why O'Leary has no reason to help me out.

You're a bunch of matchmakers trying to make the wrong match."

"Hmmm. First things first. You look at Gideon and see anger? Because personally, I have never seen him smile the way he did this morning. Real talk, dude is the most misanthropic person I've ever met, and coming from me, that's saying something. But with you he's…" Everett paused, considering. "Lighter, I think. He really *is* nicer to you."

"Please." I snorted. "That's because last night we—" I snapped my mouth shut and felt my cheeks flame.

Ev's eyes went round. "*Ohhhh.* Well, then. *Well, then.* The spark's not out entirely, is it?"

"It wasn't like that," I said, not really sure what kind of *that* I was talking about. "It was a momentary… loss of… judgement."

"I've had one or two of those," Everett said. He grinned mischievously.

"No no no. You heard what I told you about us before, right? The physical shit is the easy part. The spark is *always* there. It doesn't *mean* anything."

"It doesn't *necessarily* mean anything," he agreed. "Are you dating someone?"

"Not exactly. No. I have a friend."

"A friend?" He was back to wry amusement again. "Just the one?"

"Just the one who, like… wants… *more.*" I waved a hand. "Can we stop talking now?"

"Sorry, *no.* Turns out I'm a Lattimer after all," Everett mused, "because I'm feeling the distinct urge to meddle and provide all sorts of advice even though it's none of my business. So! Tell me about this friend. Is he… *zing?*"

I thought about Scott and his stupid text message.

"Ah, no. He's kind of the anti-zing. He called me *sunshine* today. Like, out of nowhere." I rolled my eyes. "But he's a decent guy. We have a lot in common. We've known each other for a year now. Similar careers—enough to understand but not be competitive. We both live in Boston. We like the same kind of coffee. He gives me a shot of realism when I start to get ahead of myself. So, you know, all the stuff that's maybe *better* than zing."

Everett raised a skeptical eyebrow.

"No, seriously! Would you want to be struck by lightning every day for the rest of your life? O-or feel helplessly attracted to someone when you don't even *know* them? Or would you rather have someone you liked a fair amount, who fit into your life, who was a decent person for your kid to have around, and wouldn't make you… make you…" I broke off.

"Happy?" Everett supplied.

I blinked. "What? No."

"Okay, let's go over what we know." He set his elbows on his knees and leaned toward me. "Five years ago, you met Gideon and you married him basically immediately because it felt right at the time."

I nodded.

"You have a friend named Scott, and he gave you a nickname after an entire *year* of acquaintance, and you're weirded out."

I frowned.

"But you still think Scott is the better choice of potential partner because he doesn't make you feel uncomfortable things, and he slots into the life you've carved out for yourself."

It sounded wrong when he said it like that, but I couldn't put my finger on why.

"And then, on the other side of the coin, pretty much the minute you came back into his life, Gideon offered you a place to stay, went out of his way to help you, and you two hooked up, but you think that's wrong because he deserves to be mad at you. And also, you think you don't deserve help from the people in this town because you haven't done anything to earn it, and you don't plan to."

"I… Yes. I guess." I ran a hand through my hair again. I was going to be bald by the time I left O'Leary.

"Okay, so this is where, if I'm Henry Lattimer, I'm gonna point out your logical fallacy. You ready?"

"No." I laid back on the floor and shielded my eyes with my forearm.

"Too bad, 'cause here it is. *It's not about what you deserve, Liam.*"

"Pardon?" I moved my arm so I could look up at him.

He smirked. "God, Grandpa's right. This *is* fun. Shit. Don't tell him I said that. Okay, now comes the part where I share a relevant story." He cleared his throat. "So… I was married before. My husband died."

"Oh, God! I'm so sorry. You don't have to tell me—"

Everett smiled a lopsided smile and laughed shortly, cutting me off. "Thank you, but it's okay. For a long time, I really hated talking about it because I really hated thinking about it, but it's easier now."

I sat up, resting my forearms on my knees, and nodded solemnly.

"Anyway. We were happy, Adrian and me. We had a great life. I loved him. He loved me. And he was a good person—funny, kind to children and animals. He exercised. And he was really fucking *young*, Liam. But he died anyway. And people kept saying things like, 'He didn't deserve this. You didn't deserve this. It's not fair.'"

"It's not," I said softly. "It's really not."

"But, then, maybe fifteen, sixteen months after Adrian died, there I am, strolling into O'Leary—almost literally, but that's a story for another time—and the very first person I meet in town is Silas Sloane." Everett's smile was the kind of thing that couldn't be hidden, though he tried. "Tall, built, sarcastic, smart, intrinsically *good*, sexy as fuck. And just… *zing*." He laughed.

I smiled a little.

"Me being me, I tried to fight it, obviously. It felt weird. Wrong. Like why should I get to have that *twice*, when some people never get to feel it *once*? When Adrian had died and didn't get to feel it *at all* anymore? It wasn't logical. I hadn't earned it, blah blah blah. Didn't matter. *Zing zing zing*, all over the damn place."

Everett rocked a little, his hands on his knees.

"But *nobody* deserves the things that happen to them, really, do they? Nobody deserves to die young, or to lose the person they love, or to have to make a really hard choice and give up the person they married in Vegas, or to break a bone, or lose a game, or whatever your personal tragedy might be. That's just a lie we tell ourselves so we can feel like we control shit."

"I… I guess." *Huh.*

"And meanwhile, somewhere in America, there's an asshole who steals change from the charity collection jars at the grocery store who just won a million dollars on a scratch-off, and he didn't deserve that either. Only Santa Claus keeps lists of who deserves presents, Liam."

"But…" I shook my head. "It's not just that. Gideon and I have so much history. It's impossible—"

"Nah. Not impossible. *Improbable*. But you know what else is improbable? Fucking *electricity*. Am I right? Twenty bajillion positive and negative charges working together to beam Jack Ryan into my living room? Or, know what's even weirder? My asshole cat who hates people genuinely adores my asshole grandfather who hates cats, and the feeling is mutual." He rolled his eyes. "So don't tell me it's impossible just because it's improbable, Liam, because you've got to leave room for all the improbable, magical shit in this world."

I cleared my throat. "Wow. You're, ah… You're really going all-out to win that Santa contest, huh?"

Everett leaned over the box of props, glanced around the otherwise empty room like he was checking for eavesdroppers, and whispered, "*Ho ho ho.*"

I laughed.

He didn't. "Seriously though. When you look at Gideon now, do you still feel the *zing*?"

I hesitated. There was so much *zing. Zing* for fucking *days*. But I couldn't discount logic as easily as Everett seemed to. There had to be something I wasn't thinking of.

"Knew it!" he crowed, though I hadn't said a word. "So maybe just take things as they come. Enjoy the sweet moments for as long as they last, and let yourself be happy *now*." His smile went soft and a little sappy, sweeter than all the frosting in *Fanaille*. "I'm, ah… I'm thankful every day that I did."

"You know this whole *town* is improbable," I grumbled.

"Oh, yeah. Especially at Christmas. But don't fight it, Liam. *Let the Christmas magic flow through you*," he hissed, like that creepy dude from Star Wars.

I snorted. "You trying to turn me to the Dark Side, Everett?"

"Is it working?"

I smiled. "Actually… maybe it is."

"Okay, then." Everett dusted his hands on his pants and stood. "My work here is done. Ponder the *zing*, Liam. Ponder why it's easier to accept that you don't *deserve* a thing than to accept that deserving has nothing to do with it at all. Then *stop* fucking pondering, because when the

Universe hands you a Christmas cookie, you shouldn't overthink it, you should just *enjoy it*."

He strolled out with a wink and left me sitting on the floor thinking about Gideon... and about the possibility that I could maybe grab onto some happiness for myself, at least for a little while.

Chapter Nine

GIDEON

As I drove home through the total darkness that was early evening in late December, I couldn't help but notice all the lights. Lights on every damn building in town, lights on all the trees going up my street, lights on the houses, lights on the fences. And for the first time in all the years I'd lived in O'Leary, I didn't scoff or roll my eyes —*much* —because I had at least as much Christmas shit— yes, including *lights*—thrown around my own house.

It had started a week ago with Hazel's Santa drawing tacked to my fridge. Simple enough, right? But I'd warned Hazel Christmas decorations were a slippery slope, and I'd been right.

The next day, while we were at the bakery eating cinnamon rolls topped with a level of frosting that literally gave me heart palpitations, Hazel had mentioned wistfully how pretty the little electric candles looked in the windows of the house across the street.

Sure enough, that evening someone in a red Santa suit had rung the doorbell, and we'd found a box of brand-new window candles sitting on the porch—battery operated

LED candles, no less, like someone was determined not to let me ruin her fun with talk of fire hazards and electric bills.

Psssht. Like I would have.

Okay, possibly I would.

That night, Hazel had proudly presented me with another Santa drawing for my fridge—this one kind of manic-looking and surrounded by twinkling lights that Liam agreed looked a lot like firecrackers... though he might have just been humoring me.

On Saturday, Sam had come over to watch Hazel while I worked a very long and (thankfully) quiet shift, and Liam did more photo shoots. I'd gotten home to find Hazel and Sam had decorated the trees in front of my house with ornaments made of pinecones, birdseed, and peanut butter—"Which is basically like frosting for *birds*, when you think about it, Gideon!"—and my whole house smelled like Cal's fresh-baked gingerbread cookies, since a "Santa" I was pretty sure was Parker had dropped off two dozen of them, along with a freaking *tub* of icing so Hazel could decorate them.

Liam had said, "Is it possible for a child to literally *become* sugar? This cannot be healthy," and Hazel, with a cookie crammed in her mouth, had replied, "I totally disagree," which might have been a more compelling denial if she hadn't sprayed Liam with cookie crumbs as she spoke.

That night, another Santa drawing had gone up on the fridge, this one surrounded by beady-eyed birds and an army of staring, gaping zombies with endlessly grasping arms.

"Gideon, they're *gingerbread men*," Liam had snickered, his laughing green eyes meeting mine over the kitchen island as we ate burgers. "Jesus, what's wrong with you?"

Sunday, Mr. and Mrs. Claus—aka, Bill and Dhann Nickerson—had sent over a variety of decorative pillows and blankets from the Books and More, which had resulted in a bit of a skirmish at my front door, with me insisting I wasn't opening a *mother-fa la la-ing* home for *displaced elves*, and I didn't *need* any freakin' red and green pillows or blankets in my home, and Bill telling me that Santa's reindeer had more common sense than I did, and I should get it through my thick skull that Christmas was gonna happen whether I liked it or not, so I should take the chenille pillows before he smothered me with them. He'd launched the box over my shoulder into the front hall, sending textiles exploding around the room like shrapnel from a grenade, growled *"We hope you have a Merry Christmas!"* like it was the direst threat, and let his wife tow him back down the path to the driveway.

That night's Santa had been sleeping on a red pillow, covered with a green blanket, and wearing the smuggest little smile. Since we were out of space on the fridge, he'd been taped to the cabinet, but since the piece had been captioned, "To: Gideon, Love: Bug" there was no way I was gonna protest.

Monday, I arrived home carrying boxes of pizza, only to find that an entire miniature porcelain village complete with fake snow had sprung up on my kitchen island while I was gone. Hazel was sitting on one of the kitchen stools singing Christmas carols, cuddling Fia, and moving a tiny doll through the streets of the town.

"Hey, Gideon! Look what a Santa brought!" she'd said, grinning up at me, bright red bows in her hair. "Are you okay? Why do you look so grumpy? Ooh! *Pizza!*"

In her quest for cheesy goodness, though, she'd loosened her grip on Fia, who'd darted out of her arms and onto the counter. Cue a scene from *A Godzilla Christmas*.

"Fia! *Noooo!* You just crushed the school with all the children inside it! No, Fia! Don't eat the church!" As if anyone needed further proof that Christmas was dangerous as fuck, *amirite?*

That night's Santa was stretched out flat over a tiny village, like he was a float in a Thanksgiving parade, or possibly preparing to belly flop directly onto the pointy roofs. Or, as I pointed out to Liam later, like the specter of death hovering over an unsuspecting town.

Liam had shaken his head and shoved a leftover gingerbread cookie in my mouth, but he'd laughed while he'd done it.

Yesterday, I swear, I'd thought everything had settled down. I'd arrived home to find Liam, who'd spent the day hiking up near Frank and Myrna Lucano's place snapping pictures of snow-covered scenery, cooking pasta in the kitchen. Hazel, whose teacher had emailed Liam some homework for her, was sitting at the one square inch of available island space, working on math problems. The cat was curled up on the stool next to hers.

I'd looked around the room with dawning satisfaction because there were no new decorations, and some disappointment because there were no new treats, and I'd opened my mouth to maybe, possibly mention that I'd seen Lisa Dorian in town, but also suggest that Liam and Hazel could stay in O'Leary at least through the Light Parade since they'd waited this long, when I heard a long, low *whistle.*

"What was that?" I'd demanded.

Liam and Hazel had exchanged a look.

"Santa was already here assembling it when I got home," Liam had said, holding up his hands innocently. "I wasn't sure who they were, but Sam knew them so…"

"Santa," I'd repeated, momentarily distracted by Liam

using the word *home* to refer to my house. "Wait, *what* was assembled?"

Hazel had blinked innocently and pointed toward the dining room, where a fucking gigantic *train* sped silently around a circular track nearly as big as the room itself.

"What in the he— *ho ho ho* is *that* thing?" I'd demanded, watching it chug with my hands on my hips.

Hazel, who'd followed me into the room, had glanced up at me with pitying eyes. "It's a *railroad*, Gideon," she'd said gently.

Liam hadn't been able to disguise the sound of his laughter from the kitchen, and when I'd stalked back in and given him my most irate *glare*, he'd only laughed harder, making my stomach clench in a way I'd only felt one time before… Five years ago. In Vegas.

For those keeping score, last night's Santa drawing had been sitting astride a steam engine like a cowboy on a horse. Liam had jokingly remarked that it looked a lot like *me*—at least, I sincerely hoped he'd been joking—and Hazel had hung it on the back of the front door, so no one leaving the house could miss it.

It was *ridiculous.*

It was… adorable.

And the whole thing—the way my space had been invaded, the way my control over everything in my life had been usurped, the way my town had been taken over by a bunch of Santa pod people—would have been monumentally fucking annoying if it weren't so fucking comfortable.

I'd come to a decision last Thursday, the first night Liam and Hazel had been in O'Leary, that I was going to stop being an angry asshole. Liam had left me, yeah, but it had happened after *two days*. And yeah, we'd made promises, but I couldn't blame him if he'd felt like he'd had other promises—Hazel promises—that outweighed them. I *could* be mad that he'd left the way he had, but did it really make sense to hold onto my anger longer than our relationship had lasted? Maybe him being here was a chance for closure, to end things in a healthy way.

But… while it had been surprisingly easy to let go of the anger, once it was gone there was nothing to keep me from feeling the full force of all the other emotions Liam, and Hazel too, stirred up in me.

Turned out, I liked coming home after a shift, walking in the door, and feeling the house *alive* around me. Turned out, I liked eating dinner while Hazel chattered on about some crazy thing—a documentary on hydraulic engines, a cartoon about fairies, a new person she'd met in town, the way she could just *tell* my cat was a Beyoncé fan. Turned out, it was way more fun cooking and watching television and just… *existing*… when you could look up and see a gorgeous pair of green eyes across the counter, on the other side of the sofa, or in the passenger's seat beside you.

I had to physically stop myself so many fucking times from leaning over to touch him, to pull him against me, to kiss the shit out of him. I'd promised that anything physical would be *his* call, though.

And I hadn't been lying the other day when I said I really couldn't stand seeing Liam sad.

But, the lack of sex—the lack of really any fucking physical connection whatsoever—hadn't mattered. We didn't *need* the physical because the pull between us had always been there, had never really died at all. Dormant but electric, it was as strong as it had been in Vegas.

Hell, it was *better* than it had ever been in Vegas because Liam and I had never had *this* before. We'd had heat and passion and connection, but we'd never coexisted in the same space for this length of time, taking care of the mundane tasks that make up the majority of life. Now that we were, it felt… real. I could see how our lives would play out, just like this.

Forever.

And *Jesus fuck*, who even was I right now? "Real"? "Nice"? "Forever"? I didn't believe in that shit, and I knew I was prolonging the inevitable by not asking hard questions. But *fuck*, for the first time since Vegas, I *wanted* to believe. It probably made me the biggest fool in the universe, but I wanted Liam McKnight again… and not just in my bed.

And while I was dreaming of the future, for all I knew Liam still wanted a divorce.

Rick Chang was back in town, as of today. He'd stopped me on the street to say he'd heard I was looking for him and that I could come by his office anytime. Linda Dorian was back at the library, and I'd seen Paul Fine in the window of Goode's Diner as I'd passed. O'Leary was officially overrun with notaries.

But after making a huge deal of it—to the point of *driving all the way to O'Leary to get them signed*—Liam hadn't said a single word about the papers since last Friday, like somehow after eating those cinnamon buns and setting up his makeshift photography studio over the drugstore with Everett, he'd stopped being so anxious.

Like maybe Cal's cinnamon buns were Christmas magic or some shit.

It was enough to give a guy *hope*, which was, honest to God, more terrifying than the Santa Clauses that were fucking *haunting me*.

And so, tonight I was determined to ask Liam all the shit I'd avoided asking about.

I'd texted him earlier, asking if we could go for a drive later. I was going to ask Sam to stay late with Hazel. And once we had a little calm, a little peace, I was going to ask

Liam all the things I was dying to know: about Hazel and *Scott* and what Liam truly wanted… and whether he could see forever with me too.

———

The evening went off-plan from the minute I opened my front door and a cloud of smoke drifted out. Every smoke detector in the place was blaring shrilly, from the back of the house I heard yelling, and despite a career dealing with shit a lot worse than this, my heart kicked up.

"Hazel!" I called. "Liam? Samantha?"

"In here, Gideon!" Sam yelled. "Everything's fine!"

In the kitchen, the windows were open wide, and Sam was waving a kitchen towel at the smoke detector. On top of the stove sat a baking sheet covered with the smoking, charred remains of… something. And curled up in the corner, coughing and crying in equal measure, sat Hazel Grace.

"What's going on?" I demanded, hurrying over to Hazel's side and crouching down to put a hand on her shoulder.

Hazel buried her face in her knees and cried harder.

Sam rolled her eyes and gave me a half-smile. "We were making dinner."

"Oh?" I eyed the baking sheet.

"Hazel had a great idea," Sam said brightly. "Except it wasn't supposed to go in the oven until later. When you were home. Hazel just got a tiny bit excited when I was in the bathroom and put it in the oven, and didn't set a timer—"

"It was going to be a tea party," Hazel wailed, her voice muffled.

I squeezed her shoulder gently, then turned on the

exhaust fan over the stove and opened the slider door from the family room to the back deck. Within a minute, the smoke had cleared and the blaring of the alarm stopped.

"Alright," I said, as I crouched by Hazel again. "What's going on, Bug?"

She shook her head and said nothing.

"Come on," I said. "You can tell me. What happened?" I patted her back in what I hoped was a soothing way. "Everything's gonna be fine, honey."

In one movement, she unbent from her position and launched herself at me, burying her face in my shoulder and knocking me back onto my ass. My arms went around her instinctively.

"It's *not* going to be fine! I made a *fire* in your house, Gideon! And there are all these decorations that are *fire hazards*. And I almost burnt your house down, and now you're so mad at me, and you're going to make us leave before the Light Parade, and I told Frannie and Sivan I was going to be at the Parade, and we are all going to wear sparkle dresses, and now I can't, and it's all my fault because I wasn't paying *attention!*"

I blinked. "Wow. Kiddo. That's a lot. Let's take it piece by piece, huh?"

Her breath shuddered against my neck and I patted her crisp curls as I hugged her against me.

"First things first," I said gently. "What were you making?"

"P-princess Christmas Tea Party Toast!" She sniffed loudly. "It was going to be for dinner."

I spared a thought to wonder what Liam would say about that, since "Christmas Princess Toast" didn't sound like it contained many vegetables, and the guy was gearing up to be a Scrooge about sugar since Hazel had been eating so much of it. But that was neither here nor there.

"Christmas Princess Toast sounds good," I said. I braced my back against the wall and held her firmly. "What's in it?"

She pulled back long enough to give me an implacable look, which was ruined just a tiny bit by the tear-tracks on her face. "Princess Christmas Tea Party Toast," she corrected.

"Yeah, that's what I said."

"Is not!" Her brown eyes narrowed.

"What? It *totally* is. I would never get something as serious as Tea Princess Christmas Toast Party wrong!"

"*Gid-eee-unnnn!*" Her tiny hand pushed at my shoulder, and I grinned.

"*Hay-zelll-Graaace.*" She grinned back for half a second, then her face crumpled, and she buried her head in my neck again.

"Hey, hey, hey! Bug, it's okay. It's fine. I'm not mad! See?" I pulled her away from me again and smiled hugely. "Of course I'm not. Accidents happen."

"But the fire alarms went off, and —"

"Hazel," I interrupted, tugging on one of her curls. "That's no big deal. They did what they were supposed to do and reminded you that there was a problem before a real fire could start, which means you didn't get hurt and Sam didn't get hurt and Fia didn't get hurt and your dad didn't get hurt. That's what matters. Next time, you'll pay more attention. Won't you?"

She nodded solemnly.

"So what's the big deal?" I asked. "I'm *definitely* not going to ask you to leave."

"You're not?"

"Fu… Um. *For goodness sake* no. No way. I wish… I wish you could stay longer," I finished lamely. "Long as you like."

This was so not a conversation I needed to have with Hazel. At least not until I'd had it with Liam.

"Alrighty!" Sam cleared her throat and wrapped her blonde hair in some kind of messy knot at the top of her head. "Well. I can see you two have this under control, so I'm gonna bounce. Have Liam text me if you need me Friday. And if not, I'll see you Saturday, Queen Hazel?"

Hazel nodded and stood up to give Sam a hug. "Sorry about the toast."

"Girl, not even a problem," Sam said. "Like your... *Gideon*... said. It happens." She grabbed her jacket...and my plan for a quiet, peaceful evening with Liam went up in smoke like so much Christmas Princess Toast.

"Okay," I said to Hazel, once the front door had shut behind Sam. "Now we have to clean up. You ready?"

"Me?"

"Of course. You're gonna help me clean it up, and then we're gonna make more."

Her smile was devastating. "Really?"

"Would I lie about Party Christmas Princess Tea Toast?"

"You don't even know how to *make it*." She rolled her eyes as I picked her up and set her on the counter next to the sink. "I know because I made up the recipe myself, with only a little help from Sam."

Twenty minutes later, we'd cleaned up the baking sheet, made new Princess Toast—which turned out to be baked cinnamon toast made with red and green sugar, which was just as appetizing as it sounded—and filled the kettle with water to make tea. I'd also gotten Hazel to eat a few bites of chicken and broccoli left over from the night before, which I figured offset the cinnamon sugar.

Because that was how nutrition worked.

"Do you have teacups?" Hazel asked after the kettle whistled.

"Nope. 'Fraid not. These mugs are the best I can do." I nudged the plain, blue-and-brown stoneware mugs with my fingertip.

Her mouth twisted. "They're fine, I guess. I have teacups back in Boston. They're *beautiful*."

"Yeah?"

"Yup. They were my mother's when she was my age."

I glanced down at Hazel, who was busy arranging our "tea" in the mugs—an actual tea bag she'd unearthed from some cupboard for me, scoops of hot chocolate and mini-marshmallows for her.

She'd never mentioned her mother before. Neither had Liam.

"It was nice of her to give them to you. For my twelfth birthday, I got a signed football that had been my dad's when he was younger. I still have it."

"Did your dad die too?" she asked innocently, and my heart broke a little for her… and a little more for Liam.

Shit.

"No. My dad's still alive. Your mom died, Bug?"

She nodded. "And my dad. When I was two. And I went to live with Daddy, and I was a *handful*. Pour the water, Gideon!"

"What? Oh! Right," I said, reaching for the kettle to fill the cups. "On it."

It was so unbearably tempting to ask Hazel for more information, to get answers from her to questions that seemed so hard to ask Liam.

But that would be shitty.

And besides, I wanted to hear it from Liam's perspective.

He'd taken on someone else's kid. What was that like?

I'd already seen how parenting weighed on him sometimes, but knowing he was doing it alone? Damn.

"Hazel, how old are you exactly?" I asked.

"I'm going to be eight in August, and I'm going to have a party." Her eyes narrowed. "Why? How old are you?"

"Forty in January," I answered absently, doing a bit of mental math.

Liam had become Hazel's guardian... *five years ago*.

My stomach twisted.

Why had it never fucking occurred to me that *I* should contact Liam? I'd been so fucking *hurt* when Liam left—so upset that he'd made me want him, *need* him, and then walked away—it had legitimately never entered my mind that *Liam* might need *me*. But what if he had? What if, five years ago, Liam had needed his *husband*?

"Gideon!" the tiny despot said.

"Huh? What?"

She sighed. "I *saiiid*, our tea party is ready now!"

"Right, right." I shook my head to clear it. "Hop up on the stool then, and let's chow."

She stared up at me in horror. "Hop *up*? And *chow*? Gideon, don't you know how tea parties work?"

I tucked my top lip between my teeth. "I'm afraid I don't. I've actually never been to one before," I admitted.

"Oh." She clasped a hand to her chest. "That's so sad."

"Mmm."

"Okay, I'll show you everything to do! First, we must take our fine china"—she pointed to the heavy ceramic mugs—"to the tea table. And Fiadora will join us at the appointed time."

"*Fiadora*," I repeated, looking around for the cat. "Right. Um. Which way to the tea table?"

"Come along," she said imperiously. She grabbed the

plate of cinnamon toast, a plastic container of leftover cookies, and a bag of cat treats, had me grab the "fine china," then led me to the coffee table in the living room. She sat cross-legged on one side of the table and pointed to the other. "That is *your* seat for the party."

I eyed the floor dubiously. There was a very lovely over-stuffed couch right next to it.

"Gideon, trust me," she said. "This is how you tea party."

I nodded and sank down with minimal grace, then contorted myself to fit in the tiny space I was allotted.

Hazel set out the food and arranged the mugs appropriately, then she set two or three cat treats on one of the empty sides of the table. Sure enough, Fia came over to investigate a second later.

"Oh, *Gertrude*," Hazel said in her fake British accent. "Doesn't Fiadora's new dress look stunning?"

Look, I'd never spent any time around kids before. I think that was pretty clear. So it shouldn't be a shock that I had no idea Hazel was talking to me until she repeated, more loudly, "*Gertrude!* I *said*—"

"Wait. I'm *Gertrude*?"

"Of course you are. Princess Gertrude. For heaven's sake, don't you know your own name?"

There were times, in the past week or so, when I was pretty sure I *didn't*. The lights shining in the living room window, the occasional whistle from the dining room, and the fact that I was curled on the floor in my own home suggested I'd become someone else entirely.

But I was shockingly okay with that.

"Pardon me, Princess Hazel," I said meekly. "What were you saying?"

"I was *saying* that Princess Fiadora's dress is *stunning*."

I eyed the cat, who was licking chicken cat treats off

my coffee table and seemed to be enjoying my embarrassment just a bit too much.

"Stunning," I agreed. "But not as stunning as yours, Princess Hazel. That pink-like color is... magical."

Hazel smiled, and I thought maybe I was getting the hang of this. Pretty sure I wouldn't be bragging about it to anyone, though.

"Why thank you, Gertrude!" She took a sip of her hot chocolate with her pinkie firmly in the air. "And I do adore your hat. The feathers are *delightful.*"

I touched a hand to my head. "Um. Thank you? I... plucked them myself?"

One small eyebrow raised, and she shook her head just slightly.

"I mean, thank you for that enchanting compliment, Princess." I took a sip of my tea—which was *hella* bitter, prompting me to remember that I fucking *hated* tea—and remembered to lift my pinkie also.

"Gertrude, I do so enjoy staying at your house for the holidays."

"Wait, pause," I said, holding out a hand. "Am I supposed to be doing the fake accent too? Because I'm pretty sure I can't do that."

Hazel sighed. "Gertrude, *of course* we are expected to speak in our best company voices."

"Ah." I cleared my throat. "I do so enjoy having you here Princess Hazel. I do declare, it's the loveliest gift I've ever received."

I was pretty sure I hit halfway between British and... Southern belle?

Fia jumped from the table to the couch and started licking herself, which clearly showed what *she* thought of my effort, but Hazel didn't seem to mind, so I went with it.

And I took a second to thank God that Parker wasn't

here to see this because if he *were*, he'd get that weird, gooey look on his face and possibly start to think that he had a *talent* for matchmaking.

Which he did not.

"I cannot wait for our Christmas *ball*," Hazel said. "We shall dance the night away."

"Oh. Uh. I'm sure you dance divinely. And your ball gown will be, uh…" I'd already used every adjective in my vocabulary. "Splendiferous?"

A small sound—more than a breath, less than a laugh —made me turn my head toward the kitchen. Liam was lounging against one side of the wide archway, watching us.

Christ he looked good. His cheeks were pink, probably from the cold, and his face had lost its tired look over the past week. His posture was relaxed, his mouth was twitched up in a casual smile, and his eyes were… *fuck*. They looked *hungry*.

And not for Princess Toast.

Well, damn.

In my mind, I heard Parker whisper, "*Movaries, Gideon*." I rolled my eyes at myself.

Hazel jumped to her feet. "Daddy! Guess what? I almost burned Gideon's house down!"

Liam straightened and his eyes went wide. "You what?"

"But he's not mad because it's *not a big deal*." This was delivered almost as a warning, in case Liam was tempted to make it a big deal, and I smothered a smile behind my cooling tea.

Blech.

"Some burned toast and a kitchen full of smoke. It really *wasn't* a big deal." I said, looking up at him.

"But also, Gideon said that I could stay here *as long as I like*."

Liam's eyes met mine. "Did he now?"

"Of course," I said, and I meant it to come out casual and shit, but instead it came out gravelly and intense.

"So can we, Daddy? Can we stay for longer? I have *plans* for the Light Parade, but also it would probably be best if we were here for Santa Claus. Less confusing for him that way."

Liam blinked. "That's… Hazel, that's another whole week and a bit. We can't… I don't—"

"Long as I like," Hazel repeated. "Right, Gideon?"

I nodded at her because it was easier than trying to read the expressions that flickered over Liam's face. "Sure thing, Bug. But why don't you let your dad and me talk about that first, okay?"

"'Kay!" she agreed happily. "Daddy, come join our Princess Tea Party!"

Liam's eyes softened. "Tea party with my best girl and my best…" He darted a glance at me and cleared his throat. "… Gideon? How could I say no to that?"

I would have given a lot to know how he'd been planning to end that sentence. But like with the other questions between us, I was going to have to wait for an answer.

"Get some tea from the kitchen and come sit with us!" Hazel decreed. "You can be Princess Lavender."

Liam looked at Hazel, then he looked at me. "I can't wait," he said. And I was pretty sure he actually meant it.

Chapter Ten

LIAM

SHIT.

Shit shit shit.

If there was anything sexier than hearing a grown man —a tall, muscled, crinkle-eyed, growly-voiced, sexy-as-a-*slooooow-fuck* man—chat about gowns in an accent that was half Scarlett O'Hara, half Dowager Countess of Grantham, I could not tell you what it was.

That was fucking unexpected. But then, in my wildest imaginings I could not have predicted any of the shit that had happened this week.

I immediately turned and strode to the kitchen to get myself a mug of tea, partly because I was eager to get back to watching Gideon play princess and partly because I worried I might explode if I watched them any longer. In fact, when I got to the cupboard, I stood there for a whole minute with my hand clenched around a mug handle, just breathing in and out and trying not to feel too much.

Being around Gideon for the past week hadn't made me immune to the man in any way. In fact, every minute I spent with him just made me crave the next minute that much more. And it wasn't just a physical thing, although… yeah, that was very real also. Gideon just called to me in a way I couldn't explain—not just sexual, or intellectual, or emotional, but all of that and more, the way a compelling photograph wasn't simply about the composition or the light or the speed or *any one* of those particular things, but about the magic that happened when all of those things were exactly right and created a whole greater than the sum of its parts.

I rested my head on the edge of the cabinet door. And apparently I was also a fucking poet now. A terrible one.

A terrified one.

The first few months after Nora died, I'd had to force myself not to think about Gideon. I'd be up in the night with Hazel, soothing her after a nightmare and feeling really fucking sorry for my sleep-deprived self, and my mind would immediately jump to Gideon the way your tongue worries a sore spot in your mouth. *How was he doing? What was he doing? Did he think of me? Did he* hate *me? Was he alone? Had he moved on?*

It had made me *sad*. Sad in a selfish way that bled into the whole rest of my life. I'd realized that I'd left Gideon for Hazel's sake… but I hadn't left all the way. I'd still hoped he'd find his way back to me—on a white horse, obvs—and rescue me from the lonely anxiety and the relentless day-to-day obligations of my life.

I'd been looking around for a steady, responsible adult to help me figure out what the fuck I was supposed to be doing. And then I'd realized… *Oh, shit*, that steady, responsible adult was supposed to be *me*. So I'd stopped dreaming up fairy tales—stopped myself from thinking about Gideon at all, except for the odd nightmare—until a couple weeks ago.

I kinda wished I'd taken notes on how I'd accomplished

that, since I had no clue how I was going to repeat it when it was time for us to leave here. Not after kissing him and cooking dinner beside him, seeing his face over morning coffee and laughing with him before bed.

We were supposed to be getting a *divorce*.

This was supposed to be an *ending*.

Ripping off a Band-Aid.

The next step in a whole line of tough decisions I'd made for Hazel's future.

I had a whole alphabetized, indexed list in my mind of all the reasons that was the best, most logical course of action, and if I needed convincing, I had Scott calling me and texting me ten times a day, even though I'd stopped answering two days ago, alternately telling me I was crazy, offering help with whatever "business" I needed done, calling me irresponsible by taking Hazel away from her routine, and suggesting dates when I got back to the "real world."

But deep down, this ending felt an awful lot like a new *beginning*. And I didn't want the "real world." At least not the one back in Boston. I wanted this fantasy—the little snow globe vignette where Hazel, Gideon, and I lived together, laughed together, were a *family* together—to be real, instead.

"Stop overthinking," Everett had said. "Just enjoy it. See where things lead."

Apparently, they led to me staying in O'Leary for Christmas. But after that?

Gideon and I needed to talk. Soon.

"Daddy!" Hazel called.

I took a deep breath, blew it out, filled my mug with tea, and went back to the living room.

"Lavender!" Gideon cried. "Come sit by me." He patted the ground beside him.

Lavender? Seriously?

I folded myself up cross-legged on the carpet and Gideon lifted a brow in my direction. "Showoff," he muttered.

"What?"

He waved a hand toward my legs. "You're half human, half pretzel."

"Oh." I looked down at my lap, and then over at his half-bent legs. "I guess I have more practice at this than you do. Or else I'm just bendier than you are."

Gideon's gaze burned so hot I'd swear my skin singed. "Oh, I remember how bendy you are."

My entire body flushed. He hadn't said a single flirty, sex-charged thing to me in a week, and then *this*?

"*Shush.*" I shoved his knee.

Gideon grabbed my hand and spread it out flat on his thigh. Despite the thick layer of denim separating our skin, this was the most physical contact we'd had in a week, and the bolt of lust that shot through my gut was all out of proportion to the level of contact. *God*, I wanted him.

With a single fingertip, he traced the outline of my splayed hand, coasting up the side of my fingers and gliding down into the delicate webbing between. Reflexively, my fingers curled into the thick muscle beneath them, and his breath hitched.

"So, Lavender, are you excited for the Christmas ball?" Hazel asked.

I tried to snatch my hand away from Gideon, but he grabbed my wrist and held me in place.

"Um… *Is* there a ball?" I asked. "I didn't know."

Gideon's large hand covered mine, pushing my hand into his leg like he was warning me to *stay*, and my dick twitched.

"Oh, Lavender." She shook her head sadly. "Of course

there is. All the most important people in the neighborhood have been invited. I'm going to find a prince—or possibly a princess? I'm not *totally* sure?—who'll marry me and make me a princess because that's how that works." She sighed. "Unfortunate, really, that it's not the kind of thing you can earn."

"But if it went on merit, would they have dances where ya could wear yer sparkles?" Gideon asked. His voice was definitely sliding more to Yosemite Sam than anything remotely British.

How could he be so hilariously ridiculous and so ridiculously sexy at the same time? It wasn't fair.

"Excellent point," Hazel approved.

"I, ah… I don't believe I received an invitation to the ball," I said.

"You can be my date!" Gideon said. His thumb stroked the side of my wrist. The tiniest touch, and my heart rate rocketed.

"Gertrude!" Hazel said, shocked. "You can't just *tell* Lavender she'll be your date!"

"*Cain't I?* Why in tarnation not?"

I made a gurgling sound in my effort not to laugh.

"Because if you want a date you need to *ask*." Hazel shook her head, exasperated with the ignorance of adults. "*Politely.*"

"Oh." Gideon gave me an assessing look. "I see."

"Do it now."

"Hazel!" I shook my head, somewhat embarrassed, and tried unsuccessfully to snatch my hand back again. "Gideon doesn't have to—"

"Gertrude," Hazel insisted, brown eyes determined. "And yes, she *does*. It's *polite.*"

I opened my mouth to protest, but Gideon cut me off.

"Would you go to the ball with me, Lavender?"

"Gertrude." Hazel face-palmed. "That's *not* how you do it. You really have no idea how to get dates, do you?"

I turned my lips in and bit down.

"I really don't," Gideon said solemnly. "I haven't asked anyone out on a date in… oh, five years or so."

My fingers flexed on his leg. "Seriously?"

Gideon's golden-brown eyes met mine. "Very seriously."

I swallowed. "Me neither."

"Yeah? Not even Scott?"

I shook my head, struggling to remember what Scott even looked like, let alone how I'd thought he and I could ever be more than colleagues.

"Okay, so here's what you do," our dictator said. "Gertrude, tell Lavender she looks beautiful and she's special and she's very smart. And that you would be *devastatingly thrilled* if she would consent to go with you." She waved a hand between us. "Now you try it."

I bit my lip again—I was lucky I wasn't drawing blood at this rate—and Gideon's mouth twitched. "You know, I think I'm going to have to practice a few times first. Maybe in the mirror."

Hazel nodded sagely. "Good idea. You could also consider a dance routine or something. I can send you a YouTube link."

I observed a personal moment of silence for my daughter's future suitors, whoever they might be.

"You could also consider being really honest with her," Hazel advised. "Tell her all the secrets you've been keeping."

Gideon froze. "Secrets?"

"Like, maybe, *your middle name?*"

He snorted and shook his head. "Nice try. I don't talk

about my middle name. No one but my mother knows it for sure."

"Is it Petunia? Peter? Percival? Paul?"

"No."

"Perry? Pepper? Packer?"

"Packer?" He shuddered and so did I. The horrible jokes would have written themselves. "Jesus, no."

"Pablo? Pip?"

"Gertrude, don't you find it *dreadfully* annoying when people persist in asking you questions you'd rather not answer?"

Gideon's mouth turned up in a lopsided smile. "Indeed, Lavender. *Dreadfully* annoying."

Hazel huffed and rolled her eyes but moved on.

And meanwhile, I resolved to figure out Gideon's middle name myself.

The next hour passed by in a blur. Hazel led us through a discussion of all the hot gossip in the neighborhood—mostly details of her imaginary Christmas ball—and every so often, after taking a sip of tea, Gideon would move my hand an inch up his thigh. I hadn't known a tea party could be the world's most bizarre kind of foreplay, and it felt like it should be seriously fucking wrong, but damn. It was also so, so good.

And I would never be able to taste this tea again without getting hard.

Finally, a seemingly interminable amount of time later, Hazel yawned hugely.

"Tired, Bug?" Gideon said. "Bedtime?"

Hazel shook her head stubbornly. "I would never leave in the middle of a party."

"But tomorrow afternoon, you were planning to make decorations for the Parade," I reminded her. "Don't you want to be well rested?"

She sighed. "I guess."

"Speaking of decorations," Gideon said, looking around the room with narrowed eyes, "Nothing new arrived today while I was gone?"

Hazel shrugged and traced a finger along the coffee table. "I don't know what you mean, Gertrude."

He narrowed his eyes. "No new railroads? No blow-up Santas in the backyard? No tiny re-creations of a North Pole elf sweatshop in the hall bathroom? Has my laundry detergent been replaced by something that smells like a *fa la la*-ing candy cane?"

Hazel laughed. "No! None of those things!"

"A Rudolph head hanging on my wall? Tinsel in my underwear drawer? A tree in my shower?"

"No!" She laughed harder. I realized I couldn't remember the last time she'd laughed that hard with anyone but me, and the realization broke my heart, at the same time seeing her now with Gideon put it back together again. "Though I would really like Santa to bring a tree. Just not in your shower."

"You wouldn't lie to me, would you, Hazel Grace?" he teased, leaning over to tickle her ribs.

"Of course not!" She ducked away. "Gertrude, your manners are appalling."

"And you, Princess Hazel, need to get to bed," I told her. "Shower first."

She sighed again. "*Orrrr* we could have more toast."

"*Orrrr*," Gideon said. "No more toast, and instead you come help me pick out a Christmas tree tomorrow."

Hazel's eyes widened. So did mine.

"But you said Christmas trees are fire hazards," she whispered.

"Not if you take proper care of them," Gideon said,

casting a sideways glance at me. "I think a lot of things are dangerous if you don't take care of them properly."

"I'll take care of it!" Hazel said, a huge smile dawning on her face. "*I so will.*"

"I know," Gideon said. "And so—"

Whatever he was going to say next was cut off by my daughter launching all fifty pounds of herself around the table and onto Gideon. He caught her with two hands.

"You are the best," she told him, her little arms tight around his neck. "Thank you, thank you, thank you!"

I swallowed hard, supremely glad that she was happy and also… a little sad because *shit*, I wished I'd been the one to put that look on her face.

"Don't thank me," Gideon said softly, catching my eye over her head. "Thank your dad for bringing you here. He loves you an awful lot."

"Yeah, I know," Hazel said, pulling back in confusion. "He's my *dad*. He *always* loves me the most. Even when he makes me *shower*."

I laughed, then pushed myself to my feet before I broke down and bawled like a baby. "Which is what you'll be doing now," I reminded her. "Door open, remember lotion after, and braid your hair or tomorrow-Hazel's gonna travel back in time and kick ya."

"'Kay." She got to her feet and took a step toward the front hall and the stairs, but then impulsively turned and threw her arms around my waist. "Love you, Daddy."

I ran a hand over her curls. "I love you too, Buglet."

She skipped away.

Gideon and I looked at each other awkwardly. I couldn't look at him without thinking about his hand on my wrist and my fingers on his leg, but the taking it further while Hazel was around—and *awake*—was impossible.

I grabbed a handful of dishes and mugs and walked

quickly to the kitchen. "So, I guess no drive tonight, huh?" I called over my shoulder, turning on the water and letting the sink fill with hot suds. "Probably for the best. I had a long day, and I bet you did too. I don't know if it's because it's Christmas or because people are still trying to play matchmaker, but if I could get half this number of clients back in Boston, I'd take up studio photography permanently. It's not a thing I would have thought I'd like, but it turns out—"

Gideon came up right behind me and reached around to deposit the remaining dirty dishes into the sink. My thoughts scattered.

"It turns out?" he prompted.

"Huh?"

He grinned and I stared stupidly up at him. He was possibly the warmest person in the universe, and standing next to him was a lot like sitting by a fireplace—comforting and relaxing and potentially dangerous.

"Nothing. You know, I really did want to take you out, show you some of my favorite after-dark haunts, but I couldn't ask Sam to stay when Hazel was so upset about burning toast earlier." He lowered his voice and sounded remorseful. "Wasn't a big deal at all, but it seems like I might have hit the whole 'fire hazard' thing a little hard before. Scared the shit out of her."

I shut off the water. "Gideon, you're fine. *She's* fine. If you *did* scare her, you definitely managed to reassure her, too."

He nodded slowly, his brown eyes serious, and I wondered if he would kiss me, but instead, he took a giant step away, leaning against the counter. I went back to washing the dishes under his watchful eye, and I heard the water turn on in the shower upstairs.

"What?" I finally demanded. "Never seen a person

wash dishes before?"

He shrugged. "Never seen *you* washing *my* dishes."

Oh.

Before I could think of a suitable response to that, he continued, "Hazel mentioned having teacups at home. That her mom had left her."

I paused in the act of rinsing a mug. "Yeah. My best friend Nora. She and her husband Jake were killed in a car accident."

"So Hazel's *not* your daughter."

I gave him a fierce look. "She is every inch my daughter."

"Biologically?"

I shook my head.

Gideon folded his arms over his chest and leaned his head back against the cabinet like he required support.

"Did you think she was?"

He shrugged. "I wasn't sure *what* to think. Or if it was my business to think at all."

This was the time when I could say that it *wasn't* his business. Which is exactly what I would have done a few days ago. But now, I figured maybe it was time to have a different kind of hard talk.

So I finished rinsing a mug, carefully put it in the dish drainer, and said, "Five years ago, the morning after we were… were *married*, I got a call from the Dallas police that there had been a car accident." I glanced over at him. "You weren't there."

"I was out getting us coffee." His voice was soft and remorseful, but there was no need for that.

I nodded. "I figured. I mean, later. When I was actually capable of thinking. I figured you'd stepped out and you'd be back. All your stuff was still there. But I… I wasn't thinking at the time." I cleared my throat and rinsed another mug. "You hear about people in shock not thinking clearly, but I wasn't thinking *at all*. Just one step in front of the other, emergency systems only. You know? I mean, I guess you probably must. You see people in emergency situations all the time."

He stared at me, nostrils flaring, and nodded once.

"The police said I was listed as the emergency contact in Nora's phone. They said Nora and Jake had *died*, which couldn't possibly be right. But they had Hazel—her arm was broken, and she wouldn't stop crying —and I... I had to get to her."

"Shit."

"I threw stuff in my bag, I kept calling Jake's phone and waiting for him to pick up, because I knew he and Nora had to be so scared when they couldn't find Hazel, and I..." I set the dish in the drainer, turned off the water, and gripped the edge of the sink with both hands. "It wasn't until I got to the airport that I even remembered you and I were... that I should have... that I hadn't even told you I was going." I looked over at him. "Best husband ever, right?"

His brown eyes were fierce on mine and he tilted his head to the side sympathetically.

I let out a shuddering breath. I was dimly aware of the shower turning off upstairs. "I didn't have your number. Which sounds so ridiculous now, but we'd barely been out of each other's sight for a minute, and I hadn't expected... Anyway. I tried calling the hotel, but you'd already checked out."

"I did. I thought you'd left. Left *me*."

"I hadn't." I squeezed my eyes shut for a second. "Not then."

"You left your ring behind."

My eyes flew open. "No, I didn't. Damn thing was too

big. Kept sliding off my finger. Remember?"

He shook his head.

"We talked about having the rings sized later." I shook my head ruefully. "We kinda left a lot of things to do *later*, huh? Anyway, I didn't mean to leave it behind. In fact, I was really fucking sad when I couldn't find it. I kinda wanted to have it just…"

"Just?"

"Just to have," I said lamely. To put in a box someplace safe, where I could keep it forever to remember what we'd had, and never look at, since remembering hurt so much.

"And then what happened?" Gideon demanded, arms still crossed. "You couldn't call me at the hotel. You didn't have my phone number. You left town and so did I. I get it. But I'm not *that* hard to find. You knew where I lived then. You knew what I did for a living. You could have tracked me down in a matter of days. Hours, even."

"Yeah, I could." I blew out a breath and dried my hands on a kitchen towel. "See, the thing is, once I got to Dallas I had to make, um… funeral arrangements? For Nora and Jake." I cleared my throat. Five years had passed and in some ways it felt like five minutes.

Gideon dropped his chin to his chest. "Fuck, Liam."

"Nora's brother and Jake's parents were pissed that Nora and Jake had wanted *me* to have custody. Well, not so much Robert once he knew they didn't have any life insurance, but Jake's folks were *very* hurt, and they even threatened to challenge me for custody in court, and I… Suddenly I had an actual *human* relying on me to take care of all her needs—food, clothing, shelter, emotional support. I had no fucking clue what I was doing, you know? I didn't have much money saved. Hazel wasn't sleeping through the night. The doctors said she needed consistency and routine in order to *acclimate*." I laughed without amusement and the words kept tumbling out. "How *does* one acclimate to being an orphan? And Jake's parents were horrified that I lived in a studio apartment, so I had to get a bigger place, and that meant buckling down and taking local jobs, and I… I felt like I was under a microscope. But taking care of Hazel was the last thing I could ever do for Nora—" My voice broke and I took a breath to steady it. "So what else could I do? You know? No way forward but *through*."

I turned, steadying myself with a hand on the countertop and faced him. "My entire life changed in the blink of an eye, Gideon, and I had to change from the person I was—carefree, haphazard, *irresponsible*—to become the parent Hazel needed. And it's *not* that I didn't value our connection, or think you weren't the greatest thing to happen to me up to that point, because you *were*. You… you *definitely* were. But you were the fantasy, Gideon. And I was thigh-deep in diaper-changing, toddler-tantrum *reality*. You and I hadn't discussed kids or even where we'd *live*, and I'd sort of imagined that wouldn't matter because I'd move wherever to live with you, and I'd keep traveling and you'd keep doing your thing, but I… I couldn't do that anymore. And it—" I closed my eyes and let out a breath. "It was one thing to trust that we had a future when it was just me and my happiness I was risking, but a whole other thing when it was Hazel's health and happiness on the line too. And *that* is why I didn't call you. And I'm sorry, Gideon. Truly. Not that I left, but that I did it that way. And if you ever thought, even for a minute, that it was about *you* not being enough, then I'm even *sorrier*. And I'm sorry that it took me filling out my own will and realizing that custody issues were gonna be fucked up if I was *legally married* to finally cowboy up and have this conversation and—"

Silent and sure, Gideon crossed the distance between us and cut me off by brushing his lips over mine. His thumbs brushed my cheeks, wiping away tears I hadn't even known I'd shed.

"Okay," he said, taking my hands in his.

"Okay?" My voice shook.

"Yeah, *okay*. As in, I get it. As in…" He swallowed. "I would have done the same thing."

My stomach flipped and my breath hitched. "You what?"

Gideon licked his lips. "I wish it hadn't happened that way. I wish your… *Nora* hadn't died. I wish you hadn't adopted Hazel under those circumstances. I wish we'd known each other even a little bit longer so you could have felt like you could count on me. And I wish I'd been with you when the call came in that morning because I think… I think it all would have worked out differently. That we would have faced it together. But I'm not mad that you put her first. How could I be?"

Looking at him I could see he was one hundred percent serious. "You don't… you *can't*… know what you would have done if you'd been with me that morning."

"Sure I can. I *don't* know how it would've worked out long term. And neither could you. Which is why I'm saying I think you did the right thing." He cast his gaze toward the ceiling, toward *Hazel*. "I wouldn't risk her for anything either. You're raising an amazing kid."

I sniffed. "I worry a lot about whether I'm doing what Nora and Jake would have wanted," I admitted softly. I was pretty sure there wasn't a person on the planet I'd ever admitted that to, not even Livia. "I worry I'm not enough."

"You love her like she's the most precious thing in the universe," Gideon said. "I don't think they could ask any more of you than that. In fact, that's probably why they picked you in the first place. Right?"

It was my turn, then, to kiss him. Without overthinking —hell, without thinking *at all*—I unlinked our hands so I could slip my arms over his shoulders, and kissed him with everything I had: all my apologies and my fears, all my hopes and my joys, for the person I was five years ago and for the person I was right then.

I couldn't explain what it meant to have him believe in me like that. But maybe I could show him.

Gideon moaned and leaned closer, pushing my back against the counter, spearing his fingers into my hair. It felt like coming into myself again, like the moment after you'd contorted and stretched and held your breath to take a picture and you finally relaxed and exhaled. It felt like... *zing*.

Gideon stepped back, and I had to remind myself that breathing was important.

"Come on," he said, holding out a hand, and I didn't hesitate.

He flipped off the lights and led me upstairs.

I paused by the door to Hazel's room to say goodnight, and found her already asleep in bed, every light blazing, curled next to a blinking Fia. Hazel's hair was a corona around her head, which she was going to fiercely regret when it was a jumble of knots the next day, but I didn't wake her to fix it. Instead, I pressed a kiss to her forehead, turned out all but one light, and pulled the blankets over her. When I turned toward the door, I found Gideon waiting for me.

I grinned and put my hands on either side of his waist, then I towed him the rest of the way down the hall toward his room.

Chapter Eleven

GIDEON

LIAM'S EYES WERE GREEN FIRE—THE MOST BEAUTIFUL thing I'd ever seen. I'd wanted him since forever, in the way you dream about the one person who's perfect for you, before I'd even known he existed. Fate had brought us together, and we'd fucked it up the first time around because he'd been scared and I'd been stubborn. Now it had brought us together a second time, and I'd be damned if we didn't make the most of it.

He towed me from the hall into the semi-darkness of my bedroom. The little LED candles flickered in the window, and the shadows and light played across his gorgeous face.

I wanted to fall asleep beside that face every night. I wanted to wake up next to it every morning. I wanted my second chance.

"Liam," I breathed, backing him into the foot of the bed. "I—"

He fell back on the bed, pulling me on top of him...

And the entire world erupted into holiday madness.

A tinny version of "Deck the Halls" started playing

from the speaker on my nightstand, while that stupid, *stupid* song about the grandma and the reindeer blared from somewhere else. Tiny multicolored lights flickered and flashed like disco balls all around the room. And from beneath us, the goddamn bed yelled "*Ho ho ho!*"

How the hell had my *bed* started talking?

"Jesus Christ in a manger, it's a poltergeist!" I pulled Liam upright, yanked him behind me, and ran over to flip the light switch by the door. He gasped at the sudden brightness and buried his face in my shoulder, but me? I couldn't close my fucking eyes to the horror that surrounded us.

My bedroom looked like Christmas had vomited all over it.

An entire mistletoe forest hung from the ceiling, the dressers were covered in other, different greenery. My generic, navy-blue bedspread had been replaced by one that looked like a gigantic, king-sized Santa face—big, black, vacuous circles for eyes, a gaping, red maw of a mouth, and clouds of white for his beard. And at the top, near the newly red and green pillows, stuffed animals of Santa and all eight of his goddamn reindeer lit up and *neighed* and occasionally screamed "*Ho ho hoooooo!*"

"Oh dear God. Is that Santa dancing?" I whispered.

Liam peeked over my shoulder, then buried his face against the back of my shirt again. "I'm afraid so." It sounded like he was laughing. *Traitor.*

"They have gone *too far* this time," I said, halfway between a growl and a whine. My heart was beating out of my chest. "I am going over to Parker and Jamie's house this minute, and I can only *hope* they are having sex. Fuck, I hope they're naked and about to *climax* because I am going to *knock on their windows and yell Christmas obscenities*. I will bring eight maids a'milking and however many lords a'leaping *right through their living room*, and a bunch of goddamn klieg lights too, to make sure everyone sees the show. I will bring a fucking children's choir to sing Hazel's Kiddie Bop Christmas songs with their chipmunk voices and kill any potential boner Parker and Jamie might ever have again. I will camp out on their lawn dressed as The Grinch and demand cookies and eggnog every hour on the hour, *every damn night until New Year's*. Or possibly the Fourth of July. I will…"

Liam shut me up by spinning me around, grabbing my face, and giving me a laughing kiss that had my heart beating fast for an entirely different reason.

"Or maybe," he murmured against my lips. "Maybe we could wait and get revenge tomorrow?" He kissed me again and it nearly drowned out the sounds of the singing. "Maybe you could let me take care of everything for right now."

"Take care of what?" I demanded, my mind still stuck on vengeance. "Because we could take my truck—"

He pressed his lips to mine, and when he smiled, it made me smile too.

"*You*," he said simply, and it took my brain half a minute to realize he was answering my earlier question. "Just relax, okay? You've already fought a terrible toast fire and survived tea party etiquette lessons from a seven-year-old. So just… stay right there."

I nodded once and he kissed me again. Then he moved around the room, shutting off lights, unplugging the speaker, throwing the singing stuffed animals into the closet —which only made them sing *louder* until he shut the door —and pulling the unspeakable, horrifying bedspread onto the floor.

"The, ah… the sheets appear to be reindeer print."

Liam's mouth twisted to the side. "Do you have a reindeer phobia or just a Santa phobia?"

"It's not a *phobia*." I scowled. "Did you *see* its soulless eyes?"

Liam bit his lip, but his smile came through anyway. "I saw," he agreed solemnly, coming back to stand in front of me again. "*Soulless*."

"You're humoring me, aren't you?"

He grabbed the hem of my shirt and dragged it up just an inch so he could lay his other hand flat against my abs.

"Maybe a little bit?"

"Keep doing it," I groaned.

He slid both hands up over my chest, leaving little trails of electricity in their wake, and pulled my shirt over my head.

I went to do the same for him, but he stopped me. "Look at you," he said softly. He pushed me to sit at the edge of the mattress and his eyes roamed every inch of my exposed skin, but he didn't look *happy*, he looked... tortured.

He leaned down and kissed my neck, right below the place where my pulse pounded, and his fingertips skimmed over my arms from my shoulders to my elbows and back again. He pressed a second kiss to the edge of my left shoulder, right above my armpit. He sank to his knees and pressed a third kiss to the spot just to the right of my right nipple. A fourth an inch lower. A fifth over the outside of my rib cage, just beside my elbow. And then a sixth to my right forearm.

"Liam," I whispered.

"Shhh."

He pushed at my shoulder until I was laying down on my stomach with my arms splayed to the side, then he made the same strange journey again. A kiss to my shoulder. Three sliding kisses down my shoulder blade. A long tongue-swipe along the column of my spine right where I'd gotten stitches when I … oh.

Oh.

"Liam," I said again, turning over slightly and reaching for him. "Come here."

"You got hurt," he said, resisting my efforts to pull him on top of me. "So many times. So many little scars."

"Nature of my job," I reminded him. "But nothing serious, babe. Except the back thing. That was—" I cleared my throat. "That wasn't awesome. But I'm here. I'm okay. I'm fine."

I wasn't sure if he heard me. His fingers were still trailing up and down my skin.

"I wasn't here for any of these." He whispered the words like a secret, and I wondered if he was talking to himself. "You could have *died*, and I wouldn't have known."

"Well. I mean." I swallowed. "Not exactly. You're kinda the beneficiary on my life insurance policy, so."

"What?" he demanded.

There were probably more awkward times to talk about shit like this than after you'd had a Santa-induced meltdown while trying to have sex, but I couldn't think of any.

"Never mind. It's just a technicality. Being my, ah, spouse and all."

Liam's jaw dropped. "But… but there are ways around that if you name someone else."

I shrugged, uncomfortable. "I suppose." But I hadn't bothered with any of them. I hadn't wanted to.

Liam bent his head and kissed me again, and I shivered.

"Babe, come here," I repeated. But he pushed himself

up, rolled me to my back, and covered my mouth with one hand.

"Shush, Gideon. Just… just be quiet and let me. Okay?"

I nodded slightly, helpless to refuse him, as under his spell as I'd ever been.

Liam started at my neck and worked his way down my torso again, this time kissing not only the scars but also the pleasure points. He dragged his teeth over my skin and worried at my nipple, then knelt between my spread legs and ran his tongue over each of my abdominal muscles, while I clutched the reindeer sheets like they were the only thing keeping me grounded in reality, because they *were*.

He climbed off the bed, pulled off my boots, socks, jeans, and underwear, then lavished the lower half of my body—minus my insanely hard cock, because he was cruel like that—with the same attention he'd shown the upper half, kissing not only my scratches and dings but every stupid freckle. I'd never been so aware of just how many miles of skin there were on my legs until he'd insisted on kissing every inch.

Liam nuzzled his nose into the juncture of my legs, his breath hot and moist on my balls, and I groaned. His cheek dragged against my erection, spreading the precum that pooled at the tip.

"Liam, baby," I breathed. "Fuck. *Hurry*."

He stood up and shucked his shirt, throwing it on the floor.

"What do you want, Gideon? Tell me." His voice was hoarse, like he'd been just as aroused and tortured by his kissing as I had. "My mouth? My hand? My ass? Whatever you want, it's yours." He reached for his fly and pushed his jeans down.

"What?" I propped myself up on my elbows to see him

better. The window candles glowed behind him, making Liam look like something out of a vision. The ghost of Christmas past… or maybe, *maybe* the ghost of Christmas future.

"Pretend I'm Santa Claus," he said. His voice was teasing but his eyes were deadly serious. "But not the soulless kind. You can have anything your heart desires. Just ask."

Things flashed through my mind. Hazel and her drawings and the candles in the windows. Liam petting Fia while I poured coffee. Hazel planting flowers in my front yard in spring. Liam and me watching a summer sunset.

But I didn't feel like I could say any of that, so instead I said, "*You.* Just… you."

Liam grinned. "Convenient," he teased. "Would have been *super* awkward if you'd said Ev or something." He pushed at my shoulders until I was lying flat again, then put a knee on either side of my legs. "But *how* do you want me?"

He lowered himself so our cocks slid together, and we groaned in two-part harmony.

"I want to be inside you," I said, lust thrumming through my veins too hot for me to keep silent. My cock fucking *ached* with the need to claim him. "I want to fuck you until you forget everything, everyone, but me."

He laughed, short and breathless. "Shit. Like I could think of anyone else? You think I'm reciting a list of presidents here?"

"I'm not kidding." I grabbed him and rolled so he was beneath me, then propped myself up so I could stare down at him. "I want you to forget the last five years ever happened. Forget every guy—"

"You don't listen," he interrupted. "There haven't *been* any other guys. Not since you."

I ran a hand over his forehead, pushing back his hair so I could see his eyes in the dim light. He'd said similar things before—that he hadn't dated, that he didn't date—but…

"None?"

"Not like I had an abundance of free time, and I…" Liam shrugged. "I'm guessing by your shocked expression you can't say the same?"

I wished like hell I could, but I shook my head slowly. "None since I moved here," I said instead. And the couple of guys I *had* fucked around with had been one-night stands. Simple, uncomplicated… wildly unsatisfying.

Liam leaned up and kissed me. "I get it. It's fine," he soothed.

But it *wasn't* fine. I was suddenly dying to be inside him. To be back where I belonged. To erase my *own* memories of everyone who wasn't him.

I hastily stood, just long enough to grab the bottle of lube from my nightstand, and groaned when I climbed back on the bed and my skin touched Liam's again. I poured a thick stream of lube on my fingers—way too much and with *zero* finesse because my hands were shaking too hard.

"*Fuck.*"

"Gideon," Liam said softly, grabbing my wrist. "It's okay, baby."

"I just… I want you. Badly."

"And I'm here," he assured me, lying back down. "I'm right here."

"But I want this to be perfect—" So I can keep you forever.

"It *will* be perfect. It's always been perfect."

I exhaled a shaky breath and looked at the man in my bed. Green eyes, brown hair, killer smile, gorgeous body.

But so much more than all of that. The way his gaze locked with mine said he knew I needed reassurance, the way his pulse hammered in his throat and his breath came fast said he needed this connection as badly as I did.

I lowered my head and took his cock into my mouth at the same time my fingers found his hole and slowly, slowly opened him.

Liam's eyes were wide and his skin was sheened with sweat by the time I was done. His cries rang in my ears. My fingertips gripped his hip tight to hold him in place. The salty, delicious flavor of him danced on my tongue. The scent of our combined arousal was all around us. And I thought that this was exactly what I wanted every day forever—Liam in my bed, Liam taking over all my senses. Just Liam.

"Condom," Liam breathed. "*Fuck*, Gideon. Now now now."

"Oh, shit." I sucked in a breath as cold reality invaded our happy bubble. "I… I don't have any. *Fuck*." I lowered my forehead to rest on his shoulder. "I don't *have* any. Do you?"

I felt Liam shake his head. "Five years, remember?"

Yeah, I fucking remembered. A fresh bolt of lust seared through me.

"I mean, I get screened biannually for work, and I know I don't have any…" I swallowed. "And I'm assuming you've been tested in the last five years." He nodded. "So, we could… I mean… No. *Fuck it*."

There was a lot more to going bare than just being disease-free. At least, I'd always sort of thought so. Which was part of the reason I'd never even considered it until now.

"Doesn't matter. We'll skip that for tonight."

Liam made a noise of protest.

"It's *fine*. I promise, I'll make it good for you." I bit the tendon between his neck and his shoulder. "You can come down my throat, just like the other night." My own cock twitched in anticipation.

Liam thumped my shoulder with his fist, and when I lifted my head, he scowled. "Do you realize how often we do this? Overthink shit and make assumptions?"

He pushed my shoulder, and I let him roll me onto my back.

"This is what I want," he said simply. "You. Inside me. Right now. Bare. Is that what you want?"

"Fuck yes," I breathed.

I barely got the words out before Liam had my dripping cock in his hand, lining me up with his hole and sinking down *oh so fa la la*-ing slowly without a single thing between us.

Liam riding me was fucking glorious. Delicious. A thing I'd missed and craved without even knowing I was missing it.

If anyone ever tells you that sex is sex, that a willing partner is a willing partner, that physical intimacy can't change you or fix you, trust me when I tell you they're wrong. Because the sight of Liam McKnight working me over—his eyes squeezed shut while his channel opened for me so sweetly—felt like the world's quietest revolution.

He clenched around me as he rocked up and I was lost; he sighed as he sank down, and I was found again. All the weary, bruised parts of me—all the scars that Liam's lips could never touch—felt healed suddenly, and all the doors to all the parts of my heart that I'd locked away and bricked up for the past five years were thrown open wide.

I ran my hands over his chest, fingers clenching into his damp skin, wanting to be even *closer*, and then those glorious green eyes opened. He leaned down and kissed me, sliding his tongue against mine.

Fuck.

I flipped him over in a heartbeat, pushing his legs up to his chest. "Yes?" I demanded.

"Yes," he agreed. "Always yes."

And I thought if I were ever going to write a love poem, those would be the only words I'd ever need. I was so giddy, so fucking *joyful*, that I grinned at the idea.

"What?" He tried to frown, but it was like my smile compelled him to smile too, because his lips twitched. "We're stopping? Why the fuck are we stopping?"

I ran my hand over his cheek and shook his head. "You make me so…" I shook my head. What was a word that was deeper than happy? Sturdier than joy? "You make me *glad*."

Liam's eyes widened, then fluttered shut when I pushed inside him again. I took a minute to appreciate the perfection of it—Liam's legs around my waist, his hands gripping my neck—then I leaned back up on my knees and got to work, remembering how much he loved it when I took him over, found the perfect angle to stroke his prostate with every thrust, and forced pleasure on him.

"Fuck, Liam. *Fuck!*"

Liam's hair was in his eyes, his lips parted as he breathed out "*Gideon*," and I wanted to promise him anything, give him *everything*, keep him just like this, as close as this, forever.

His ass clenched around me as he came, shooting all over his chest and his chin—and, with any luck, the goddamn reindeer sheets—and then I was coming too, filling him up and he cried out again.

"Oh, God, that feels…"

"*Perfect*," we said together.

I dipped back down to kiss him, then collapsed at his side, catching my breath.

"I feel," I said, a short time later, as I ran my finger through the pool of cum cooling on his chest, "that there's a joke to be made here about mountains of frosting."

"But you won't make it," he said sounding very severe and also slightly drunk. "Because that would be *bad*."

"Or maybe it would be *excellent*," I mused. I ran my nose into the sweaty hair at his temple. "Maybe I'll look back on this moment and regret losing the opportunity."

"Remember those revenge plans you worked out against Parker and Jamie?" he said lazily, rolling toward me just slightly and insinuating his leg between mine. "Erection-melting Christmas displays?"

"Yeah." I held him tighter and buried my face in his hair. "Why? You threatening to set up decorations on my lawn? Because honestly? I don't care if you have every milkmaid in O'Leary out there—"

He laughed. "*Are* there milkmaids in O'Leary?"

"Liam, I have no idea what Henry Lattimer gets up to in the privacy of his own home, okay?"

He laughed harder.

"But it doesn't matter how many people camp out on the lawn or what kind of carols they sing, I can't imagine not wanting you, so don't even bother." I swiped a finger across his chest again and smiled smugly. "And apparently the feeling's kind of mutual, considering how *mountainous* this level of fros—"

"I know where the dancing Santa is," Liam whispered.

"What?" I laughed weakly. "*Please*."

"And all the dancing reindeer too."

"You wouldn't—"

"No! Of course I wouldn't!" he laughed, waving a dismissive hand. "Gosh, no, Gideon! Imagine reindeer bells shaking on your dashboard every time you start the engine? Imagine Santa Claus shouting *ho ho ho* from the shower every time you use the toilet? That would be... It would be... *cruel*, really. Wouldn't it?" He paused and pulled back just slightly, enough for his green eyes to meet mine. "Or maybe... maybe it would be *excellent*. Maybe I'd look back and regret missing the opportunity."

I pressed my lips together for a second, fighting laughter. "You're a devious man, Liam McKnight."

"I know."

And I was in love with him. I was pretty sure I'd never stopped.

I ran a hand down his flank, and he trembled against me, which made me want to kiss him. And the beautiful, beautiful thing about this moment right here was that *I could*.

So *I did*.

Chapter Twelve

GIDEON

"HMM. IT'S *A* LOOK," HAZEL SAID, PURSING HER LIPS and tilting her head as she considered one of the many, many Christmas trees Ross Landscaping had set up on the empty baseball field behind the elementary school. "But it is *the* look?"

I folded my arms over my chest. "Hazel Grace, how many other trees have we looked at?"

"Fourteen."

"And you've rejected…"

"Fourteen."

"Because they were too big or too full or too naked or too smug." I shook my head. "Still don't know how a fu —*fa la la*-ing tree can be smug."

"Look at it," she commanded, pointing at the tree behind me, which looked a little lopsided, like it was standing with its hip cocked out. "*Smug.*"

"Fine, okay. It's… smug," I allowed. "But that's still fourteen trees you've rejected—"

She shook her head sadly. "Make that fifteen. This one's just too… pretty."

"How can a tree be *too* pretty?" I demanded. "Isn't prettiness actually a good quality in a thing you plan to sit and *stare at* for hours on end?"

"That's a very shallow way of looking at things," she said with such droll sincerity that I couldn't really be impatient… except, no wait, I actually *could*.

"You can look at three more trees," I began.

"Thirteen," she shot back.

"What? *Five*."

"Twelve."

"Hazel."

"Fine, eleven. Because that's a good compromise," she said happily. "You're almost as good at this game as Daddy."

"Ten," I said. "Because I'm better at this game than he is."

"Absolutely." She turned to Angela Ross, who was standing at the cash register nearby, along with Micah and a guy in a Santa costume and beard I figured was Constantine. "Ms. Ross, where are your best trees?" she called. "Not the prettiest ones but the ones with personality? I'm going for a certain aesthetic."

An aesthetic. Jesus.

Angela flipped her black braid over her shoulder and grinned at Hazel. "You know, I think I have *just* the one you want at the end of this row. Come see if it's the right fit."

She held out a hand, Hazel took it, and they walked away, chattering happily. I shook my head as I watched them go.

"You're sunk," Micah said gleefully. "Kidlet's got you wrapped around her finger."

"Who, me?" I turned to look at him. "Nah. It's fine. I play the compromise game *well*." Better than Liam.

"Dude," Con said, pulling down his white beard. "She just got you to agree to look at ten trees when you said *three*. You might be better than Liam, *possibly*, but my money's on Hazel every time."

I scowled. He might have had a point. Still… "She's a good kid. She's just got a thing for trees. Actually, all Christmas decorations." I paused, considered, cleared my throat. "And tea parties."

"Tea parties?" Con laughed. "Tell me she's got you sitting on the floor sipping tea."

I shifted my weight from one foot to the other. "I like tea." I *hated* tea.

"Con, baby, while you're mocking Gideon over there, did I or did I not find you sitting out in my sister's backyard a few weeks back, wearing a sparkly, horned headband and drinking pink soda with Olivia?"

Con ducked his head so he could glare up at Micah from under his eyelashes. "That was a *unicorn* party, Micah. *Jesus Christ.* Totally different."

"Ah," Micah said, nodding. "Apologies."

"Besides, I'm not mocking Gideon! *Much.* I think it's adorable." He winked. "I think *Gideon and Liam* are adorable."

I rolled my eyes as another Santa Claus came sauntering up and bumped Con on the shoulder in greeting. "Oooh, Gideon's dishing about Liam? I arrived just in time."

"Parker, your hat is tilted," I said, gesturing to his perfectly straight hat.

"Is it?" He reached up to straighten it and ended up knocking it off-kilter. "Better now?"

"*Mmm.* Much."

Micah ducked his head and snorted.

"So, Gideon's picking out a *Christmas tree*." Parker

hopped up on the makeshift counter next to the register. "Clearly something cataclysmic has happened. It *could* be that the end times are upon us, it's true. A rift in the space-time continuum. *Or* it could be that Gideon's cold, black heart has been tenderized by the meat grinder of *looove*." He wiggled his eyebrows and grinned hugely.

"Wow, Parks," Con said. He leaned against Micah, who wrapped an arm around his shoulders. "That's some imagery right there."

"Seasoned with the angst of your years apart," Parker continued, staring dreamily at the sky. "Roasted by the flames of a *desperate sexual attraction*, nestled on the pillowy white bun of a happily ever after—"

"Coated with the gooey cheese of Christmas magic?" Micah's voice was dry.

"Salted with a heart attack-inducing level of *annoyance* because my friend is a *dumbass* who should stick to making *hamburgers*." I folded my arms over my chest.

"Wait. *Wait.* Gideon!" Parker gasped, hands pressed to his chest. "Did you just admit we're *friends*? This is a *moment*. We're having a *moment* right now."

I rolled my eyes while Con and Micah laughed.

"Christmas miracles do exist," he whispered, saccharine sweet. Then he hopped off the counter. "Also, I *do* think I need a hamburger. I'm helping out here, and then I'm helping Jamie prep for the Parade tomorrow, and the kids'll be devastated if Santa collapses from malnutrition. Anybody want, while I'm making 'em?"

Con and Micah both nodded. "Oh, and maybe a couple for our other Santa's helpers?" Con smiled winningly. "Julian. And Daniel. And my mom. Joe Cross. Pete Daley. And, ah… Silas?"

"How many Santa wannabes do you have running around here?" I demanded.

"I dunno. Six? Eight? Ten?" Con shrugged. "The contest got way better turnout than we expected. It's amazing."

Fucking *weird* was what it was.

Parker rolled his eyes. "Burgers for a crowd. Got it. Gideon? Some for you and Hazel?"

I shook my head. "Gotta get back. Liam's home editing photos this morning, but he promised Hazel over breakfast that we could decorate the tree this afternoon. Assuming Hazel finds a tree on this lot... or in the forest... or in the universe... with the right *aesthetic*." I snorted softly.

Parker grinned behind his Santa beard. "This is your life now, my friend. Get used to it." He slapped me on the shoulder. "At least you have Liam to go home to, right?"

I nodded and summoned a smile, but I wasn't quite sure it was convincing.

Liam and I had talked a lot last night. Enough for me to know beyond a doubt that I was in love with him. And Liam... I felt pretty sure he might feel the same way.

But love hadn't been enough for him before. And I was really fucking afraid it wouldn't be enough now either.

Parker's eyes narrowed on me. "Oh! Hey, Gideon, I had a question for you about, um... fire safety. Walk with me for a second?"

Fire safety? I shrugged. "Sure. Lemme see where Hazel is first—"

"My mom's got her," Con said with a wave of his hand. "You're not going far."

I nodded and followed Parker down the long row of trees to the sidewalk.

"Alright, spill," Parker said, once we were out of earshot of Con and Micah. "Tell Dr. Parker what that face was for."

I frowned. "What face?"

"Aw, now. Dr. Parker doesn't like it when you pretend not to know what he's talking about."

"And *I* don't like it when Parker refers to himself in the third person. Especially when he's wearing a freakin' Santa costume and beard." I shuddered. "Not sure which is creepier."

Parker rolled his eyes and pulled his beard down so it hung beneath his chin. "There. All better. Now tell."

"It's nothing. Everything's good. Everything's *great*." I hesitated, rubbing the back of my neck. "I just realized I'm waiting for the other shoe to drop, that's all. Like, how can it last? Who the hell would choose this place when he could live anywhere? Right?"

"Lots of people could. *I* did." Parker's face softened. "You're legit in love with the guy, aren't you?"

I swallowed and thought about waking up to Liam in my bed this morning—the sheets all twisted around us, his leg thrown over mine like he'd attempted to climb me in the night, a little drool escaping his mouth, his head on my bicep cutting off circulation to my hand—and the bone-deep contentment I'd felt knowing I was with my favorite person ever. It had been anything but perfect, but it was *real*.

"Yeah," I said. "I am."

"And did you tell him that?"

"No." I snorted. "Shit, Parker. What kind of idiot just goes around telling other people how they feel when they don't know for sure how the *other* person feels, and they don't know whether the other person wants something permanent or something that lasts about as long as a… as a fucking Christmas tree? That's like skydiving without a parachute. Scary as shit."

Parker chuckled. "Never a truer word, my friend."

"Also as scary as tumbling half-naked into a bed

covered with dancing, talking *Santas.*" I gave him a sour look. "So thanks for that."

We'd reached the end of the tree lot I slowed my steps as we turned toward Weaver Street.

Parker laughed. "Tell the truth, the mistletoe was a nice touch, wasn't it? Silas's idea. He's a romantic at heart. Jamie came up with the dancing Santas."

"Of course he did," I grumbled. "Your boyfriend and I are gonna have words."

"Nah, think of it this way, you'll be like Pavlov's dog now! Every time you hear a Christmas carol you'll have an overpowering need to get naked and you'll be all…" He held up his hand palm down, then flicked his wrist up and whistled. "Every time. Even in April."

"Terrific. *Helpful.* I've always wanted to be brainwashed into getting an erection every time I hear 'Grandma Got Run Over by a Reindeer.' That's not troubling at all."

Parker doubled over with laughter.

"I'm plotting revenge, FYI. It's only thanks to Liam that I'm not leading a brigade of elves to your house right now for a round-the-clock drum circle to ensure you and Jameson never have sex again." I braced my hands on my hips and watched the traffic pass on the street, idly wondering just how upset Liam would be if I ran over and got Hazel a treat at *Fanaille*, and how quickly I could make him forgive me in the end.

"Liam, who you're *in love* with," Parker teased gently, his eyes still watering from laughing so hard.

I blew out a breath. "Yeah, him."

"Uh huh. And you do know one of you has to speak first, right? I mean, unless you're willing to keep feeling the way you're feeling right now for the next twenty years—"

"I'm aware, Parker," I shot back. "I just—"

"Hey!" A tall, good-looking guy in an orangey sweater

bleeped the locks on the dumbest-looking, smushed-faced, black-and-white BMW I'd ever seen—if a little VW Bug and a giant Suburban got drunk and mated, they might produce this offspring—and lifted his hand in greeting.

I blinked. Even in O'Leary, we tended not to wave at people we didn't know, and the guy's plates said he was from Massachusetts.

"Oh. Yeah. Hey," Parker called, waving in answer because he was friendly like that. "Have a nice day."

I said nothing, but I watched the guy walk across the street to Micah's Blooms with narrowed eyes.

"Tourists," Parker sighed once the guy had disappeared into the flower shop. "I loves 'em and I hates 'em. But frankly, I love them more than I hate them because—don't tell Jamie—we're getting a cat for Christmas, so we're gonna have another mouth to feed. Julian has an abandoned cat at the clinic who gave birth to six kittens a couple weeks back."

"Yeah? Don't tell Hazel unless you're looking to have her camp out on your back porch or move into those rooms above the bar. Assuming your termites are gone?"

He coughed. "Yeah. Such a weird thing about those termites, man. Weather got cold and they all just... evaporated?"

"Uh huh. Evaporating termites. Sounds legit." I found myself fighting a smile. "Go make your burgers, Hoffstraeder. I'll see you tomorrow at the Parade."

"You definitely will." Parker gave me a salute and started to turn toward his bar.

"Oh, hey, Parks?" I called.

"Yeah?"

"Your hat's crooked again," I said. I reached up and straightened it.

He grinned hugely. "Thanks, man. Later." He darted

up the sidewalk, then called over his shoulder. "Remember to have that talk!"

"Yeah, yeah," I mumbled under my breath. I'd have the talk. Eventually.

I jammed my hands into my jacket pockets and turned back toward the school.

"Hey!" The tourist guy, now holding a giant bouquet of red and white roses, darted across the street and waved at me again.

If the dude thought I was waving back, he had another think coming.

"Help you?" I was proud of myself for only growling slightly, but I didn't stop or slow down.

"Yes!" He smiled with huge, white teeth that were a little too flawless to be anything but veneers. "I'm looking for a man."

So many potential responses to that, like, "*Oh, honey. Aren't we all?*"

Except… I wasn't. I'd already found my man. I just had to make sure he actually *was* my man.

"They have apps for that," I told Mr. Veneers, deliberately misinterpreting him because it amused me.

We hit the edge of the school grounds and I kept walking, eager to find Hazel and get home. But when I took a deep breath, I had to admit I found the pine scent was actually kind of enjoyable. I would never, *ever* understand why some people had a Santa obsession, but I could almost understand the fascination with decorated dead shrubbery, fire hazard or not.

"Not *any* man, a specific one," Veneers said, double-timing after me. "The woman in the flower shop was *completely* unhelpful."

I imagined "the woman" was Micah's sister, who'd always struck me as a really nice—if somewhat aggressively perky—person. "Maybe because she doesn't live in this town, and doesn't know who you're talking about? Or because her job is to sell flowers, not to find people? Or maybe because she has valid concerns about other people's privacy and isn't sure whether you're a deranged stalker?"

"Gideon!" Angela waved from the register at the far end of the lot. "We have a tree! Come see."

Thank God. I lifted a hand in acknowledgement.

"I'm not a *stalker*." From behind me, Veneers sounded massively affronted. "*You* just don't have *good cell service*."

I turned to look him up and down. He wore extremely tight navy-blue pants with thin rust-colored stripes, shiny brown shoes with pointy toes, a light-blue button-down shirt, and a rust-colored sweater. His hair was floppy in a way that looked casual but had probably taken thirty minutes and five products to achieve.

He was good-looking. Very. In fact, almost *too* good-looking… And wow. *Shit.* Now I kinda got what Hazel was saying about trees being too pretty.

"For the record," I told Veneers, "if I was going to be a stalker, that's *exactly* what I would wear and exactly what I would say."

The guy's face darkened and, yeah, sure enough, those good looks faded fast. "I have no idea what Liam was talking about. *Friendly fictional town,* my ass."

I blinked. Had he said… Liam?

Before I'd managed to connect the dots, Hazel came running down the path toward me, her curls and her coat flying open behind her. "Gideon, I got *the* perfect tree! If *you* were a tree, you would be *this* tree! Come see!"

Veneers turned, and when Hazel caught sight of him, she stopped.

"*Scott?*" Her face turned stormy. "What the *fa la la* are you doing here?"

"Hazel!" I said reflexively. "Language." Then I realized what I was saying and shook my head. I was losing my mind.

So this was Scott. *Liam's* Scott.

My stomach churned in instinctive, possessive denial. Liam didn't *get* to have a Scott. Liam was *mine* the same way I was his.

Except, you know… maybe he wasn't. Not for the long haul.

"Why, hey there, Bug!" Scott said. "Your dad invited me to come visit. He knew I missed you guys, and he said I needed to see this town to believe it! So, here I am!" He sank into a crouch that I swear made his pants squeak and held out his arms like he was waiting for Hazel to run into them.

Instead, she folded her arms over her chest exactly like me and gave him a dead-eyed stare. "What did I tell you about calling me that name without permission?"

Scott's smile slipped for half a second before he managed to steady it. He braced one hand on his knees to stand and clutched his flowers tighter. Then rolled his eyes at me. "Kids, huh?"

I frowned and once again deliberately misunderstood. "Mmm. They really do make the best judge of character."

"Gideon, can we go home?" Hazel interrupted in a small voice. "I'm really *quite dreadfully tired* and Daddy's waiting."

Scott's gaze cut to her, maybe noting her use of the word *home*, then back to me. His eyes narrowed and he gave me the same slow once-over I'd given him.

Scott's smile hardened. "I'm looking for Liam McKnight."

"Yeah? He's not here."

Scott rolled his eyes impatiently. "But clearly you know where he is."

"Clearly," I agreed. "But I don't know if he wants *you* to know."

"The man *invited me*. Would you like to see our texts?" Scott extracted his phone from his shirt pocket and smiled down at it. "Or maybe it's better if you don't. There are a lot of personal things in there."

My throat went tight as I stared at Scott.

Liam had said flat-out he wasn't dating anyone and *hadn't* dated anyone. He'd said he hadn't been with anyone in *five years*. And there was no way on earth he'd lie about that.

But I remembered, too, the way he'd blushed when Hazel had mentioned Scott.

The way she'd mentioned Scott fixing Liam's collar.

The way Liam had said Scott was a "really nice guy."

The way Hazel had asked Liam if they could stay until Christmas, and Liam hadn't actually said yes.

Could Liam and Scott be more than strictly friends? Yes. They definitely could.

And because I knew Liam, I knew he wasn't *in love* with Scott because he would never have slept with me if he was. I also knew from the way he looked at me, the way we acted around each other, that it was very possible—actually, really *likely*—Liam loved *me*.

But… I knew for a fact that wasn't enough.

Liam had been in love with me five years ago— or thought he was anyway—and he'd *still* walked away so he could make good, practical, *rational* decisions where Hazel was concerned. Giving her the best possible life and the best possible opportunities was the most important thing, as it should be.

So, really, what were the chances Liam would pick up

and move to O'Leary, New York—a place without takeout dinners or fancy private schools, a place where half the neighbors dressed as Santa two weeks of the year and spent three weeks a month planning, preparing, or celebrating some festival or another—on the basis of a week spent stuck at my house?

I couldn't think of anything *less* rational.

And while I'd leave O'Leary to be with Liam and Hazel in a heartbeat—though yes, fine, I'd probably miss these idiots like crazy—why would Liam even want that? I didn't fit into his life in Boston. I didn't have a job there. I loved Hazel, but I didn't know shit about raising children. And I was *nobody's* idea of a nice guy.

Hazel came to my side and slipped her hand into mine, tugging gently. "I found the tree, Gideon," she said in the same small, completely-not-Hazel voice. "So we can go."

"Sounds great," Scott said, smiling hugely. "I'll follow you."

I took a deep breath and let it out. Liam really fucking hated when people made decisions for him, right? Being manipulated by Parker and the rest of the guys had pissed him off. So the best thing I could do for the man I loved would be to give him the chance to make his own decision about this.

"You know what, Bug?" I said, running a hand over Hazel's hair. "Why don't we *not*? Why don't we let your dad and Scott catch up alone, and we can join them later?"

She looked up at me with big brown eyes. "But the tree—"

"Will be fine," I assured her, my heart breaking a little as I wondered if they'd still be around tonight to decorate it. "I'll grab it and put it in the truck. And in the meantime, why don't you ask Angela if you can go see the new *kittens* Julian has at his clinic."

Hazel shook her head. "Not right now."

I put my palm to her forehead. "Are you sick? I said *kittens*."

"Yeah, but—" She looked at Scott.

"And after you see the kittens, we can go to *Fanaille*."

She looked up at me again, clearly worried, but she nodded. "Okay, Gideon. If you say so."

Hazel giving in that quickly was a sign of distress if I'd ever heard one.

"1223 Markham," I told Scott. I rattled off directions—it was a quick right and then a left, which seemed doable even for an asshole in a dumbass car—and tried not to notice Scott's smug, triumphant little smile as he turned and left.

"So." I forced a smile for Hazel's benefit. "Where's this perfect specimen of Christmas tree?"

"Down at the end of that row." She pointed with considerably less enthusiasm. "It's got a tag that says 149. Want me to show you?"

I really wanted a minute alone.

"Why don't you go get Angela, ask her about the kittens, and ask her to send one of her Santa minions down to find me and the tree, so they can help me wrap it up. Can you do that?"

"Gideon." She rolled her eyes. "I'm *seven*."

"Hazel Grace," I shot back, tweaking her nose. "I *know*."

Her lips twitched, then her face broke out into a genuine smile and she threw her arms around my waist. "'Kay. See you in a minute," she said as she ran off.

Like the other two or three times she'd hugged me, it took me a minute to remember how to breathe around the protectiveness and gratitude that swamped me.

And it killed me to think…

Whatever. I just *wouldn't* think. I'd wait and see what Liam decided.

I stalked down the path toward Hazel's tree like the ground beneath my feet had offended me by existing and stopped when I saw a yellow tag with 149 on it. Then I stood back to assessed the tree, then took another step back… and another… until I was practically sitting in the tree behind me.

Despite my shit mood, I couldn't help smiling.

The thing was fucking *massive*—nearly ten feet tall— and I was pretty sure we'd have to get creative with some pruning because this beast was already gonna be kissing my living room ceiling, even before Hazel put a star on top.

I stepped closer to put my hand on the trunk. *Shit.* At the base, the thing was nearly a foot in diameter—I had no clue how we were gonna fit it in one of the dinky stands they sold at the Imperial—and we were going to have to buy out every package of lights between here and Rushton.

It was a logistical fucking nightmare.

It was also absolutely perfect.

The branches were full and thick, but they didn't fall into precise triangular patterns. Some stuck out too far, and some were a little short. Some looked like they'd been broken off—not surprising, since I couldn't imagine transporting this tree without dinging it a little—but it didn't make it any less *real*.

"Real, not perfect," I said under my breath. "The kid knows how to pick 'em."

"She sure does," a deep voice said way too close to my ear, and I turned to see a bearded Santa as tall and broad as I was, standing right behind me, holding a hacksaw.

Fuck. Like *that* wouldn't haunt my nightmares.

"Christ, Silas." I turned back around so he wouldn't

see the way my hands had clenched like I was ready to attack him. "Don't sneak up on a guy, man."

He chuckled, even deeper than his usual deep voice. "Sneaking's kinda my line of work."

I frowned. I didn't often think of police work as being sneaky, but okay.

"You getting a cold or something? Should you be out here coating the trees with your virus germs?"

"You know," he said, coming around me to lift the tree out of the stand, "trees like this are usually meant for a special purpose."

"Yeah?" I scrubbed a hand through my hair and fought to keep my tone civil. I hated chit chat, and I *really* hated it right now. "Didn't know you knew that much about Christmas trees."

"Oh, I make a point of knowing a little about a lot of things!" he chuckled. "Like, for instance, it's rare for a tree farmer to let a tree get this big. Most folks like 'em smaller or have smaller houses."

"Uh huh."

He set the tree down on the ground remarkably gently —the thing had to be way lighter than it looked—then crouched down and got to work cutting a few inches off the bottom, which I vaguely remembered was important for the tree to absorb water in the stand.

"Most of the time, trees get cut down after seven years, maybe less. But a tree like this has to be at least twelve years old."

"Fascinating. Truly. Everett's life must be so enlivened by these little fact-filled discussions." I leaned back against a large tree behind me and crossed my arms over my chest.

"Ah, Ev's a good boy," he said heartily.

I blinked. *A good boy?* That was *way* more than I ever needed to know about Si and Ev's sex life.

"You know, sometimes things need an extra five years or so to really mature, to get to where they need to be," he continued.

I scowled. "Are we still talking about trees?"

"'Course. What else would we be talking about?" he said innocently, still busily sawing at the tree trunk.

"You need me to help with that?" I asked.

"Nope. All under control. So why don't you tell me what's gotten you even crankier than usual on this fine day, Gideon. Tummy trouble, maybe? Too many sweets? Too much frosting?"

I narrowed my eyes. There was no way he could know about the *other* frosting thing. There was no way *anyone* could know.

"My stomach is fine," I said shortly. "I just…" I blew out a breath and admitted, "Liam's friend's in town unexpectedly. He says Liam invited him."

"*Hmm*. Is that likely? For Liam to have invited him here when he's staying with you? That'd be kinda rude, wouldn't it?"

Huh. "I guess it would." And Liam never wanted to put me out. I hadn't thought of that. *Why* hadn't I thought of that?

"*Hmm*. And what did Liam say when he saw his friend?"

"I… I don't know," I admitted. "He just showed up here in town, so I directed him to the house."

"So your husband supposedly invited a friend to town, to possibly stay in your house, but didn't tell you he was coming *or* give his friend the address."

I frowned harder. "When you say it like that, it sounds—"

"Odd? *Hmm*."

"Enough with the *hmm*," I grumbled. "He had text

messages from Liam, okay? They're friends, but Liam blushed when he was talking about the guy. Liam thinks he's *nice*."

I sounded like a jealous idiot. I *was* a jealous idiot. I couldn't remember ever being jealous of anyone or anything until Liam came into my life and common sense deserted me.

Silas was silent for a minute. "Do you think Liam thinks *you're* nice, Gideon?"

"I'm *not* nice."

"Not what I asked," he said gently.

I looked down the seemingly endless row of trees. Did Liam think I was nice? I snorted. Maybe. I was nice *to him* usually. And to Hazel. Because I hated to see them unhappy. Maybe that counted for something.

"People are a lot like trees in that way, aren't they?" Silas went on. "What's right for one isn't right for another. Lot of people would see this tree and think it was too much trouble. Lot of effort to go through for a hunk of dead shrubbery, eh? Logistical nightmare. Would've been better —easier—if it had gotten cut down oh, say, five years ago."

I stared down at Silas's bent head. Was the man a fucking mind-reader?

"*Buuuut* then, for the right person, this is the exact tree they need." He made a harrumphing noise. "Unless of course, the tree is a jealous idiot who convinces himself he's too much work and lets that *one right person* go on his merry way *for the second time in five years* and doesn't even tell the person he's in love with him or *try* to make things work."

"Pardon?"

"Nothing, nothing," Si said. He chuckled lightly. "Just mixing my metaphors. Terrible habit."

"Hey, you've got some crucial facts wrong, okay, buddy? Liam left *me* back then!"

"And *you* didn't go after him." Silas stood up and brushed pine needles off his pants. His bright blue eyes met mine. "And maybe it would have worked out, and maybe it wouldn't, but you didn't want to take a chance any more than Liam did, even though all *you* had to risk was your *pride*. You really wanna make the same mistake twice?"

"I'm trying to let him make his own decisions!"

"But how can he make the *right* decisions when he doesn't have all the facts?"

I stared at him blankly for a minute. "I guess... he can't."

Si shook his head. "Nope, he can't. So, then...?"

"I've got to get home." I ran a hand over my head. "Right away. But first I've gotta get Hazel, and pay Angela, and haul this beast to the truck."

"I'll ask Angela to let Hazel stay here for the afternoon and drop her back home later. They'll both love it. And I'll get the tree out to your place too."

"On your own?" I shook my head. "You can't possibly—"

"I promise, I can."

"I owe you one, Si." I shook his shoulder lightly.

He winked and shoved gently at my shoulder. "Go, Gideon."

I jogged down the line of trees toward the exit, and when I looked back half a minute later, Silas and the tree were gone.

Chapter Thirteen

LIAM

I SHUT THE SCREEN OF MY LAPTOP AND PUSHED BACK from the desk in Gideon's office with a sigh. I'd gotten edits done on nearly all the Christmas portraits I'd taken so far, and I'd even had time to work on a few of the shots I'd taken while I was out hiking the other day. I wasn't sure whether they'd make it into the collection I'd planned to assemble, but it didn't matter. There'd be other collections.

I couldn't remember the last time I'd felt so *good* about a day when I'd done so little. But I liked it.

I'd woken up in the darkness and felt Gideon's arms around me as he snored gently in my ear. All the Christmas lights in the neighborhood had been turned off, the entire house had been silent—not a single dancing Santa or prowling kitten to disturb the peace—and for half a second, I'd felt restless, not because I'd had something I needed to do, but because I'd thought I *should*.

There *had* to be something to do, right? There was *always* something to do. Emails to check, Hazel's homework to review, paperwork to fill out, pictures to edit, phone calls to make, presents—so many presents—to buy, things that needed to be thought about, and rethought about, and decided on. Hazel was outgrowing her boots, we were outgrowing our apartment, my boss was distinctly Scroogey about my extra time out of town, and the guy behind me was two hundred pounds of overthinking waiting to happen.

But the bed had been warm, my pillow had been comfy, and my phone had been downstairs. I hadn't wanted to disturb Gideon or move even one millimeter away from him. And as I'd lain there, I'd noticed I had a clear view of the indigo sky and a smattering of twinkling stars above the house across the street. I'd stayed as still as I could, hardly breathing, and watched as the world changed around me. The stars winked out. The sky got darker, then lighter again.

I'd started thinking about what Everett had said the other day. About how deserving things didn't matter sometimes. About how we feel like we have to carve out places for ourselves in the world, to carve out the parts of *us* that don't fit in the world… but no one ever tells us when it's time to stop carving. We end up strip-mining ourselves and wonder why we're depleted.

Everett had said to take things as they came, and I'd legit even tried to do *that* actively, white-knuckling my way to happiness like there was a way to objectively measure how well I was doing it. Like there was a way to objectively measure how well I was doing *life*.

Down the hall, my daughter was cuddled in bed with a cat, dreaming that Santa was real and plotting world domination, and when morning came, she was going to go pick out a *real, live Christmas tree for the first time ever, Daddy*. The guy I loved was holding me tight, and whatever happened tomorrow or the next day, I had that *right now* when I'd thought I'd *never* have it again. I had work to do in the morning that I enjoyed. I was warm, and full, and in need of a shower. Christmas was coming.

I was happy. Hazel was happy. Gideon was happy.

And that was *enough*. That was *everything*.

So I'd fallen back to sleep.

When I'd woken up again, I'd carried that peace with me. And while I would probably always think of the night I'd met Gideon as the best night of my life, last night had been a close second.

The night I'd met the love of my life, and the night I'd realized I could actually keep him.

I heard a car door slam out in the driveway and I smiled to myself, psyching myself up for the next few hours of full-on-Hazel tree-decorating mania. I ran down the stairs and reached the hall just as the doorbell rang.

I grinned as I threw it open. "Did you forget your key, or do you need my—"

"Surprise!" There was a dark-haired guy in the doorway holding a bunch of roses when I'd been expecting a silver fox with a pine tree.

My smile fell. "Scott? What are you doing here?"

"Rescuing you!" He stepped forward and leaned in to kiss my cheek, but I took a quick step back. Unfortunately, that meant Scott ended up in Gideon's hallway.

"Rescuing me from what?" I very deliberately did *not* shut the door.

"From whatever *business* is keeping you from getting back to Boston." He stepped to the middle of the hall and did a three-sixty, frowning at the ride-on railroad in the dining room and the Santa-tastic decor before turning back to me. His hair flopped over his eye. *How had I ever found that attractive?* "I've missed you, sunshine."

"Uh. Scott, I think we may have gotten off track here—"

"I know! That's why I'm here to help, so you can get things done. Judy is *not* happy that you haven't been taking assignments, and between you and me, she's started reassigning your stuff to Claudio, and he's *good*." Scott shook his head appreciatively, then seemed to catch himself. His smile looked forced. "I mean, you are too, sunshine! *Obviously*! But you don't want to start a whole *thing* where people see how good his work is and then they look at *yours* and they start to think… Well, *you* know."

I frowned at him. Had he always been like this? Talking ninety miles an hour and saying jack shit? So concerned with appearances and not with quality?

He came toward me and set his hands on my shoulders. The rose bouquet bopped me in the head, and he laughed when I flinched. "The way you smile makes me melt, you know that? It always has."

Smile? *What smile?*

"I really *did* miss you. And I know you have to be *dying* to get back to real life. You know, since you've been gone, I've been thinking about how well we complement each other. You make me laugh, I help you with your work—" He pulled me toward him.

"Scott." I pushed his hands off me and stepped far away. "Not all criticism is helpful, FYI. And I'm still stuck on how you got here. And why you thought you'd be welcome."

He blinked. "You invited me."

"I didn't."

"You did!"

"*Oooh*, that's a definite no."

"You said, 'you have to see O'Leary sometime.' So I picked now." He beamed and stepped toward me again. "This way you'll be home for the holidays, and we can—"

"Scott!" I interrupted. "Focus. You didn't have the

address for this house. And I haven't answered your texts in *three days,* so I know I haven't given it to you."

"I know, and I'm very put out. But you can make it up to me." He looked around again and set his bouquet on the table by the door. "So. Do you have much stuff?"

"Huh?"

"To move out." He stepped close enough to ruffle my hair, and once again I stepped away.

"Stop following me around like we're doing the motherfucking two-step! I am not moving out." Hell, I hadn't moved *in* yet... but I wanted to. Gideon had said Hazel could stay as long as she liked, right? And we were a package deal. "In fact, I might stay in O'Leary permanently."

"In this tiny town?" Scott's face squished up like he'd eaten something nasty. "You've literally lost your mind, haven't you? How many fingers am I holding up? Who's the president?"

"Get your fingers out of my face before I break them." I was channeling Gideon, and it felt *really* fucking good.

"Every man over twenty in this town is dressed up like Santa Claus, Liam! The inmates are running the asylum here! And I'm sorry to say it, but Hazel is *even ruder* than last time I saw her."

My mouth went dry. "You saw Hazel?"

He nodded. "At some little Christmas tree... marketplace." He waved a dismissive hand. "And that *friend* of yours who was with her is the most tactless, insulting *jackass* I've ever had the displeasure of meeting."

My heart banged crazily in my chest. Only one person I knew in O'Leary fit that description. "You met Gideon?"

"Is that his name?" Scott rolled his eyes. "You need to ask yourself, Liam, if that's really the sort of influence you want around your child."

I thought of Gideon calling Hazel "Bug" and sprawling on the rug while doing his truly horrible accent. Smiling as he hung picture after terrifying picture of Santa Claus on every vertical surface in his kitchen and letting his entire house be taken over by decorations. Taking her to buy a Christmas tree and letting her co-opt his cat into her super villain sidekick. Answering a hundred and two questions before breakfast. Saying *fa la la* twenty thousand times a day.

He *was* the kind of influence I wanted around my child.

He *so* was.

And Scott was a judgmental *asshole* who needed to get gone.

"Couple things you need to know, Scott." I advanced on him angrily and Scott's eyes widened. "First, Gideon is a firefighter. He's fucking *brave*. He puts *his* safety on the line to make sure *other* people are safe. Second"—I took another step toward him, shepherding him toward the open door—"he is one of the best people I have ever met in my entire life. He is *kind* and he is *funny* and he knows how to love in a way I don't think you'll ever be capable of, which is really fucking sad for you. Three, I do not *need* your help. I do not *want* your help. My career was going fine before you ever asked me out for coffee. And most important of all,"—I took one more step so Scott was standing on the threshold, nearly out of the house— "Gideon is *not* my friend, *he's my fucking husband*. So you can take your snotty, know-it-all ass out of his house, and out of his town, and out of my life. Got it?"

"But I… but you…" Scott gaped like a fish, which was really fucking satisfying.

"No more calls. No more texts."

"But you *invited me*," Scott insisted. "Liam. *Sunshine…*"

"I think *my husband* was pretty clear, Scott." Gideon's mild voice from out on the porch made my stomach flip in the best possible way. "Why don't you remove yourself from my property before I have to remove you?"

Scott turned to look at Gideon and his eyes widened even farther. He swallowed. Then he turned back to me. "Fine. I'll go. But if I walk away, that's it—"

"Yes," I said, throwing my hands up in exasperation. "That's exactly what I'm hoping for here."

"Excuse me," Gideon said, pushing Scott out of the way. He walked into the house, locked the door behind him, and turned to me. His tawny eyes were lighter than I'd ever seen them. "Say that whole thing again," he demanded.

I licked my lips. "Which part? The part about going away?"

Gideon shook his head. "Definitely *not* that part." He stepped toward me, and I took a step back, but this time I didn't really want to get away, which was handy since he caught me and pinned me to the wall by the door.

"The part about you being a really brave firefighter?"

He grinned and slid his hands down to my wrists, then slid my wrists up above my head. "Shoot, I missed that part. You can definitely repeat *that*… but later."

"The, ah… the part where I said you're the best person I've ever known?"

His features softened, but he shook his head.

"The part where I called you my husband?" I whispered.

Gideon's eyes slid shut, and he pulled in a deep breath before resting his forehead against mine. "Yeah, baby, that one. Tell me that again."

"I actually have a *lot* of things to tell you, *husband*. But I —" Belatedly, I looked around the hall like I expected a seven-year-old chatterbox to suddenly appear. "Wait, where's Hazel?"

"With Angela at the tree lot." He nuzzled my neck with his nose, then slid farther until his lips were brushing my jaw. "Probably forcing O'Learians to consider trees with the right *aesthetic*. We have a couple hours." He pulled back to nip at my chin. "That long enough to tell me all the things you have to tell me?"

"Long enough to start," I allowed.

He grinned... and then his eyes caught sight of something on the table by the door and he scowled. "Stay right here."

I nodded but otherwise didn't move as Gideon picked up the bouquet Scott had brought and chucked it out the door.

"I guess Scott left? Or did he get a face full of rose petals?"

"He's gone," Gideon said. He kicked my feet wider to give himself more room and took up his spot again. The way his pelvis fit against mine in this position was a goddamn thing of beauty, and I couldn't help pushing against him. "The flowers are on the lawn. And since they're predicting light snow tonight and *heavy* snow Sunday"—he grinned—"*I* predict we'll find the remains of those flowers in the spring."

We would. I really liked the sound of that.

But Gideon misread the tension in my body. "I mean... assuming we're still living here then," he said, his eyes on mine. "Pretty presumptuous to think you'd give up everything in Boston to move *here*, but maybe after school—"

I lifted my head and cut off his foolishness with a kiss. "You said, the first night we were here, that maybe there was a place where the things I wanted to do and the things I *had* to do could overlap. A happy medium. And I think maybe that place is here. In O'Leary. And it's not a happy medium, it's just... happy."

"This isn't some kind of Christmas hallucination, right? You're not the Ghost of Christmas-Possible making a visitation?"

I laughed. "I don't think Christmas-Possible was one of the ghosts, baby. But no, this isn't a dream." I shoved at his hands until he moved backward, then I slid my arms onto his shoulders. "Do you know, I love these shoulders? One of the first things I noticed about you." I ran my hands over the top of his sweater, loving the way the muscles gave and bunched beneath my fingers.

He snorted, his hands clenching the sides of my sweatshirt at my waist. "Always wanted for my body. It's a curse, really. No one seems to care about my dazzling personality…"

He was joking, of course, but he was serious too, and I didn't get why.

"And you use these shoulders to do the best things, Gideon. To help people who need you. To protect your town. To comfort my baby when she cries. To hold me when I sleep. And I think I knew even five years ago that I could rely on them, I was just too scared to listen to my gut. You're a good man, Gideon Mason. And I don't want to be without you again."

"*Fuck*, Liam."

He leaned against the wall by the stairs and drew me against him, sliding his lips against mine. The taste of him was familiar and exciting every damn time, and I wanted to sink inside him.

Instead, I pulled back.

"Wait," I said breathlessly. "Wait. I need to say the tough things, or I'll never remember to say them, and I… I need you to know that *I love you*, Gideon. I don't know how the *hell* it's possible for me to love someone as much as I love you. And it's so big and crazy and… *improbable*"—I grinned, thinking of Everett—"but it's the only thing that's real. So this time, for the *last* time, I want us to do this right. I want us to talk about all the things that scare the shit out of us. I want to know all the trivial shit about you and the big things too."

"Wow," he said. Then he fell silent for a minute, his face contorted in pain, like he was overcome with emotion.

"Gideon?" I said gently.

"Shhh. I'm trying not to make a joke about the *big things* I can show you, Liam, because then you're going to threaten me with those dancing Santas, and the whole moment will be ruined."

"Did I say *best* man?" I demanded, feigning outrage. "I meant *worst*. Absolute worst." I pushed him backward up the stairs, and he went, laughing and pulling me along with him.

"Good thing you love me," he said softly when we got to the top of the stairs.

"Good thing I do," I agreed. I pushed Gideon into his bedroom. "Good thing I *like* you too."

Gideon stopped and put his strong hands on my jaw. "You like me, huh?"

"More and more every day," I told him honestly, and somehow *that* seemed to get to him more than any other declaration of affection.

"Okay, you want to talk about the tough things? Then ask me, Liam," Gideon said, wrapping his arms around me. "Ask me why I never divorced you, all these years, even as pissed off and hurt as I was. Ask me why I never changed my insurance policy."

I swallowed, taken aback by the sudden seriousness in

his tone and the way his eyes locked on mine. "W-what? Why?"

"Because I was never, ever going to get married again. And do you know why?"

I shook my head, and my hands coasted up his chest to rest at his shoulders, drawn to them as I always was. "Why?"

"Because deep down, I knew nothing could ever be better than what we shared, even if it only lasted hours. I knew even if I let myself fall for someone else, it would be a pale imitation of you and me. And that wouldn't be fair. I couldn't pretend to give my heart to someone else when you were already walking around with it in your pocket."

Gideon leaned down so his forehead rested against mine.

"And way deep down? I believed that someday you'd come back to me," he said softly.

I nodded, blinking a bunch of stupid tears out of my stupid eyes so I could see the man I loved. "I'd very much like to come back to you, Gideon. Me *and* Hazel."

Gideon squeezed his eyes shut, and when he opened them a second later, they burned.

He stripped off my sweatshirt and jeans and pushed me down on the bed, and I only laughed a little *tiny* bit when his eyes darted around the room like he hoped nothing would start spontaneously dancing.

His eyes narrowed at my laughter and he shucked his own clothes in record time, then jumped on top of me, straddling me on the bed so his thick cock rubbed against mine through our boxers.

"Is this what our marriage is going to be like from now on?" he demanded, rocking slowly.

"*Fuck*," I groaned. "You mean your cock rubbing against me all the damn time? God, I really, *really* hope so."

"I mean the two of us making inappropriate jokes and laughing while we have sex."

I bit my lip and pondered this. "Yep. All the times when you don't catch me coming out of the shower with that intense look in your eyes and get on your knees for me," I agreed. "Or the times when you don't make me cry because you're so damn beautiful and I love you so much. Other than those times… yeah. It's gonna be inappropriate jokes and fucking."

"Good," he said. Then kissed me again, exploring my mouth with his tongue like he was as addicted to my taste as I was to his.

The thought came back to me from earlier that there was no right way to do this life thing, and no right way to do this marriage thing either. And so, for us, it would be laugh-sex and way too much sugar, in this tiny, absurd, beautiful town.

Later, when I was hard as a fucking *rock* and nowhere near laughter, after Gideon had slid off my underwear with his teeth and made me sing half the "Hallelujah Chorus" with his talented, *talented* tongue, he slid inside me and showed me just how much he loved me with hot, whispered words and clenching hands. And when we came together, deep in my heart I heard a *zing*… and it sounded like coming home.

———

I laid my shower-damp head on Gideon's shoulder in a place I'd reclaimed as my own. One I'd never willingly give up again.

His fingers trailed up my spine, making me shiver and press my still-interested—fucking *perpetually interested*—cock against his hip, but sex three times in one day was enough for me, coming out of retirement as I was, and my ass was still thrumming from the last go-round after Hazel finally fell asleep practically *in* her spaghetti at the kitchen counter, so instead of making a move to take it further, I yawned hugely.

Christmas tree decorating wasn't for the faint of heart.

Christmas tree decorating when your husband and daughter had brought you home a *fa la la*-ing *redwood tree* was an exercise in madness.

My hands were still sticky and smelled vaguely of tree sap, and I expected them to stay that way until February. I'd pulled more pine needles from Gideon's hair than I'd thought humanly possible. I'd marveled at the way the light companies sold the strands pre-tangled, right out of the box, to ensure maximum frustration. And we still hadn't gotten the ornaments on, since Fia kept taking each one down and then *killing it dead*.

But I'd laughed so hard my stomach hurt.

And for once, I'd enjoyed every moment of the process —the smiling ones *and* the frustrating ones—because in twenty years, when I looked back on this day, I wasn't gonna remember the tree, only the people gathered around it.

My *family*.

A gift I didn't deserve but had gotten anyway.

"Hey, Princess Lavender?" Gideon said lazily, his fingers dragging over my skin.

"Oh, no." I lifted my head. "Nope. You're not doing this."

Gideon's hand cupped the back of my neck and pushed me back down on his shoulder.

"Lavenderrrrr," he sang.

"No! *Gideon*! This is the least sexy thing ever," I

moaned. "I will never be able to have sex in this bed again."

"Lavender, you're so very beautiful."

"You know how you feel about Santa Claus and his soulless zombie eyes?" I complained. "That's how I feel about being called Lavender while we're naked."

Gideon brushed a hand across my forehead, pushing back my hair. His fingers trailed along my scalp and I shivered. "You're so fucking smart, Lavender."

I sighed and buried my smile in his chest.

He lowered his head and nipped at my bottom lip at the same time his hand traced the seam of my ass, spreading his cum into my skin, which was… okay, it was legit the hottest thing in the known universe, even if he *did* call me Lavender while he did it.

"And I want to spend the rest of my life—*our* lives—showing you just how special you are."

His words were a breath against my skin, and he lifted my chin so our gazes met, held, burned, and melted into tenderness.

"You want me to go to the ball with you?" I demanded. "Because I will so go to the ball with you. Especially if you let me sleep now."

He shook his head solemnly. "I'm looking for something more permanent than a ball."

"Yeah?" I smiled and stretched against him lazily. "Like what?"

"Like… Marry me, Liam."

I snorted. "*Oooh*, pretty sure I already did. *Kind* of an overachiever that way."

"No, I mean… *marry me*, Liam." He picked up my hand where it rested against his chest and slid something onto my left ring finger.

"Holy shit! Is that…?" I sat up and peered at my hand

through the glow of the window candles, then my eyes sought his. "Are you kidding me right now?"

"Nope." He held up another gold band, just like the one on my hand. "You left yours in Vegas. I brought them both home."

Because deep down he'd known we'd need them.

Well, *fuck*.

I took the ring he held up and slid it on his finger, then buried my face in his neck and let out a very masculine sound that was half laugh, half sob. "Okay, that's enough. No more being sweet today. I've had all I can take."

Gideon's laugh rumbled through me. "Buckle up, buttercup. Not done quite yet. I would be *devastatingly thrilled* if you would live with me forever. If you and Hazel —and any other kids we decide to have—would be my family. If you'd handle the Santa-crazed idiots of O'Leary with me, and eat mountains of frosting with me, and decorate the house with a disgusting amount of fire-hazard Christmas shit with me—"

"Eat Thanksgiving at your non-existent dining table with you?" I teased, propping my chin on his chest and wiping my eyes. "Handle all the vipers that might end up in our HVAC system with you?"

"God forbid."

"Listen to Kiddie Bop Christmas *over and over and over* with you?" I dug my finger into his ribs.

He snorted. "Wow, Lavender. You're really not selling this thing, you know? I might have to rethink."

"Too late. You *love* me," I told him.

His smile was bright enough to light up the night. "I really, really do."

Epilogue

GIDEON

Weaver Street was a mob scene.

O'Learians crowded the streets decked out in the obscenest Christmas-wear I'd ever encountered. I was so used to seeing people dressed as Santa Claus by now I wondered if I'd even *recognize* anyone after New Year's. My eyes were assaulted by red hats, green coats, striped pants, polka-dotted scarves—and that was just Henry Lattimer's wardrobe.

"Morning, Gideon!" he called from his position in front of the hardware store. He had a broom over his shoulder like a bayonet and kept one eye on the overcast sky at all times, standing guard against any potential snowflakes that might fall and attack his sidewalk. "Morning, Liam! Miss Hazel." He tossed her a wink that made her giggle.

"Morning, Henry," I said as we got closer. "Happy... Parade Thing."

Henry didn't reply at first. His eyes were glued to the sweater just visible beneath my open leather jacket. "Is that...?"

"Mmm," I agreed. "A Christmas sweater. Hazel picked

it out for me last night at the store when we were getting tree lights."

"But it's…" He stared at the reindeer dancing under a disco ball, searching for an adjective. I raised an eyebrow, daring him to comment.

"*Beautiful?*" Hazel said encouragingly.

Hen looked from her, to my sweater, to Liam, who was tucked under my arm and could barely contain his laughter. His old face went soft and his mustache twitched. "It's beautiful, alright."

Hazel beamed. "You know," she said, apropos of absolutely nothing, "Daddy and Gideon are *married*. But I can still call Gideon *Gideon*. For now."

Hen's eyes widened and his gaze ping-ponged between us again. "That right?"

Liam grinned and nodded. "Yep, Hazel and I are gonna be sticking around for a while."

"A *permanent* while," I corrected, pulling him fractionally closer. He rested his head on my shoulder and his wool hat—which was my wool hat—scratched my chin.

It was hard to imagine being happier than I was at that moment.

"Morning, Hen!" Joe Cross stepped up on the sidewalk carrying a thick stack of red and green papers. "If you're standing out here, you mind handing out these…" He looked at me and did a double take, like he hadn't recognized me at first, then looked down at the papers in his hands. His eyes widened. "They're printed on recycled paper," he blurted. "I'm not trying to kill the earth!"

I bit the inside of my cheek and held out my hand. "Can I see one?"

Joe hesitated, like he wondered if I was toying with him, but he couldn't figure out how to refuse.

"Secret Santa distribution," I read. "What's that?"

"All the details were on the other fly—" He cleared his throat. "Never mind. Silly me. It's a little thing we're doing after the Santa contest. Secret gift giving. Mostly for the young ones, you know? Folks who're giving a little something extra to make sure everybody has new toys this year. Teenagers who wanna give a present to their secret crush. That sort of thing."

"Ah. Too bad I didn't take your flyer last week then, hmm?" I looked down at Liam. "I don't have a single present for my secret crush."

"First, I'm not a secret anymore. And second, I have all the gifts I want." Liam leaned up to press a kiss to my cheek and when he settled back against me, his arm tightened around my waist. "But that sounds like *so* much fun," he told Joe.

"Yeah?" Joe's smile brightened. "Maybe you can help run it next year! Hey, Parks!" he called, waving over our heads. "Liam's running the Secret Santa next year!"

Liam's enthusiastic agreement helped me stifle my inner groan, and because I was filled with the magic of Christmas—or possibly an excess of gingerbread pancakes and bacon from Goode's Diner, which was basically the same thing—when Joe said goodbye I told him, "Patriots chances look pretty damn good this year, huh? Brady's arm is on fire," and his face went so shiny-pink with joy, it lit up the cloudy morning.

Who said you had to be mother-*fa la la*-ing Santa Claus to give good presents, am I right?

"Morning, everyone," Parker said when he joined us a minute later. He sounded breathless, like being Santa was taking a lot out of him. Or maybe it was carrying the big, black sack he deposited at his feet.

I tilted my chin down at it. "Please tell me there are no more costumes in there."

"Nope." He grinned. "Presents for the Secret Santa. All the Santas in town have been collecting them, and now *I'm* collecting from *them*."

"That's a lot of Santas," Hazel said.

No shit, kiddo.

"Which means there's a lot of presents," Parker said. "And I have even more at the bar. You guys are coming to the contest judging, right? Half an hour, out on the fair-grounds?"

"We're making our way in that direction," I agreed.

"I want to see if the *real* Santa is there," Hazel said rubbing her hands together. "I'd love to have a chat with him."

Liam and I exchanged a look over her head, and Liam shrugged. "Hazel's *decided* Santa is real," he informed Parker.

"Good call, Hazel," Parker approved. "Magic happens."

God forbid. I made a noise somewhere between disagreement and disgust, and Liam slapped my abs lightly.

"The irony of having my two favorite people obsessed with Santa in completely different ways is not lost on me," he sighed. "This is my life now."

"It's not an *obsession*," Hazel and I said together. Then we looked at each other and burst out laughing.

"Next year you'll be up there with us, Liam." Parker wiggled his eyebrows. "Won't that be *fun*, Gideon?"

"Fun," I deadpanned as Liam laughed into my chest. "Can't wait."

I made a mental note to talk to Liam about this. I'd do anything to make the man happy, but our bedroom needed to remain a Santa-free zone.

"Hey, Hazel!"

I looked over my shoulder. Julian Ross's long, gray coat

flapped in the breeze as he jogged across the street from the vet clinic, and Daniel Michaelson strode a pace behind him, kitted out in Santa-red velvet.

"Lilly and the kitties say hi and thanks for visiting with them yesterday."

Hazel grinned. "I *loved* seeing the kitties!"

"You can come back and see them another time, then. And feel free to take home one… or *three*." Daniel gave me a sickly-sweet smile.

"Wow. That's *way* too generous," I said, narrowing my eyes. "By a lot."

Julian laughed and scratched at his bristly jaw. "Daniel's trying to find them all homes before I give him my big eyes and tell him what I really want for Christmas is some new furry family members."

"I cannot resist those big, blue eyes, baby." Daniel wrapped both of his arms around Julian's waist from behind. "And you know I *love* our crew. But we've rescued *six* cats, two dogs, an owl, and a chameleon in the last *year*. I feel the need to, you know, *share* the love. Spread it wide."

"That's a delightful sentiment," my husband said. "But spread it elsewhere."

"I don't even want another cat," Hazel interjected.

I looked down at her in surprise and she shrugged.

"Not right now, I mean. Fia would be jealous. She's still just a kitten herself, and she's not ready to be a big sister yet."

"Smart," Julian approved.

"Me, on the other hand, I'm *super* ready." She grinned coyly up at Liam and me. "And I still have a free spot on my Christmas list!"

Liam coughed, and I felt my face go hot. "Ah… Maybe wait and ask for that next year, Bug," I choked out, patting her shoulder.

Hazel shrugged, unconcerned. "Santa will take care of it. So, Julian! Next time I come by, can you show me the snakes?"

Julian frowned. "The… oh. *Those* snakes." He and Daniel exchanged a look, then both of them glared at Parker, who seemed to suddenly find the gray sky compelling.

"Actually, tough news there," Julian said. "They, um…" He shrugged helplessly at Daniel.

"Ran away," Daniel supplied sadly. "No note, no forwarding address, nothing."

"Ran?" Hazel's eyes narrowed.

"Slithered," Julian corrected. "Daniel means they *slithered* away. I think they, um, got tired of Daniel's terrible flute playing."

"Hey!" Daniel protested, pulling Julian in tighter. "No more impugning my flute playing, Julian Ross, or I'll stop practicing altogether."

Julian jammed his elbow into Daniel's stomach, making him chuckle.

"That's so sad," Hazel said worriedly. "It's dangerous for vipers to be outside this time of year. They're cold-blooded, you know."

Julian's smile softened. "I know, sweetie. But I think they'll be fine. Maybe they hitched a ride to Florida. Or Arizona."

"Definitely Arizona," Parker said sagely. "Might give my mom something to talk about besides my dad's golf games."

"Just in case, I'm going to make them some little hats and scarves," Hazel announced. "Once we move my craft kit here from Boston. Daddy, can we do that soon, just in case?"

If Liam thought there was anything funny about the

idea of tiny viper hats and tiny viper scarves, he didn't show it. Instead he nodded solemnly, bent down to cup her chin in his hand, and said, "Sure thing, Bug. We'll get it right after Christmas," serious as a heart attack.

And I couldn't say why that made my chest tighten and my fingers clench into fists, overcome with the need to protect them both against anything and everything that might harm them, but it did.

At least, I couldn't explain it until Parker, that dumbass genius, leaned toward me and whispered, "That, my friend, is you discovering your *movaries*."

I blew out a breath, frustrated more than anything because I had a sneaking suspicion the asshole was right.

"Just remember who was right about you being a Daddy type."

"Not the same thing, Parker," I growled. "Not by *miles*."

"I keep telling you, it's a *vibe*, man."

"Parker? Don't you have somewhere to be? A contest to lose? A guy of your own who needs you to whisper sweet nothings in his ear?"

Parker's smile turned smug. "Your concern for Jameson is touching, Gideon, and I'm gonna go and tell him all about it right now. The bromance between you is the stuff of legends. I find myself *almost* jealous." The soul-deep satisfaction in his eyes said he was nothing of the sort.

"You know, Jamie and I have lived in this town together for *years*," I reminded him. "We got along *fine* before you showed up."

"Nah, you *thought* you were fine," Parker informed me. "You just didn't know what you were missing."

And as Liam resumed his spot at my side, I thought maybe Parker was right about that, too.

"Nice sweater, by the by," Parker said, picking up his sack again. "Are those reindeer *dabbing*?"

I had no idea what he was talking about, so I glared at him until he smacked me on the shoulder, winked at Hazel, and walked off.

"We need to hurry," Hazel said, tugging on the hem of my jacket. "The contest will start soon."

"Go on, then," I told her, waving her in front of us. "We'll follow you."

When we passed Jamie and Parker's bar, right near the fairgrounds, Silas in his Santa suit was holding the door open for his boyfriend to step out. Once he did, Everett threw an arm around Liam and hugged him.

"You drank the Kool-Aid too," he said happily.

I had no idea what the heck he was talking about, but clearly Liam did because he darted a glance up at me, and his cheeks turned red.

"The Kool-Aid was surprisingly tasty, after the first sip," he confirmed.

Everett grinned. "I'm glad. So you're here for good?"

I nodded, and Liam added, "We're moving our stuff next week, and we'll have Hazel enrolled at the school after the New Year."

"Awesome!" Everett held up a hand for Hazel to high-five. "I'll be your art teacher, then. Welcome to O'Leary."

"Art is my *favorite*. Well, after science," Hazel amended. "But let me ask you, what do you think about textiles for serpents as an art medium?"

Everett blinked. "Uh. I… can honestly say I've never considered it. But I'm ready to hear more."

I shook my head as Hazel slid her mittened hand into the hand Everett offered and followed him toward the fairgrounds.

I was thinking Hazel would be good for O'Leary. But more importantly, O'Leary would be good for Hazel.

Liam, Julian, and Daniel started chatting as they walked—something about Daniel's upcoming novel, which was a sequel to the book he'd put out the year before. I hadn't read it, though given the excitement on Liam's face, I was pretty sure I wouldn't be able to say that for long.

But I put a hand on Silas's arm, holding him back a pace so the others could walk ahead.

"Look.." I blew out a breath as we stepped off the sidewalk and onto the thin layer of snow that covered most of the fairgrounds. "I'm shit at this stuff, but… thank you. A lot."

Silas frowned. "I didn't do anything."

"Yeah, yeah." I waved a hand. "I know you didn't *really*. But all those ludicrous tree metaphors actually kinda hit home for me. Of course, in the end Liam didn't want anything to do with Scott"— and yeah, that memory made me grin—"but he still needed me to, you know, *share* and stuff. To stop being a jealous idiot who cared too much about my pride, or however you said it. I appreciate you being honest with me."

"Gideon." He shook his head. "I haven't said anything meaningful to you."

"Of course you have." I scowled. "Yesterday. At the tree lot. Maybe it didn't mean shit to *you* and *you've* forgotten all about it, but it meant something to *me*, okay? And frankly, it was really nice of you to get the tree home for me too. Where'd you get the stand? They don't sell that kind at the Imperial."

"Bud, lemme stop you right there because I *literally* have no idea what you're talking about." Silas stopped walking. "I wasn't helping out with the trees yesterday. I was *supposed* to, but I got called into work for a couple hours, and then Ev and I helped Hen hang some more lights outside the shop for the Parade."

"Wait. Wait, wait, wait. It wasn't you?"

He shook his head. "Definitely not me."

Then… who the hell had it been? My mind dredged up and dismissed everyone I knew who'd taken part in the contest. None were as big as the guy from yesterday except Silas… and possibly Daniel, although I was pretty sure Daniel didn't have light-blue eyes.

"Silas!" Everett called from ahead of us. "Babe, come on! They need you on stage with the others!"

Silas flashed him a thumbs-up, then looked at me in concern. "You okay?"

I frowned. "Yeah. Of course. I just got confused for a second there."

Silas nodded. "Well, enjoy the Parade, okay? And remember to cheer for me in the contest. The voting is done based on audience approval."

"Yeah. Sure," I agreed.

And suddenly I was *very* eager to see all the participants so I could figure out who the hell had played Dr. Phil for me the day before.

I caught up to Liam while Si jogged over to the group of Santas congregated near the stage. I picked out Daniel and Constantine Ross in the mix. Everett and Hazel strolled over to join them, Hazel still chattering about something I hoped, for Everett's sake, wasn't still fashion for reptiles.

Liam's arm slid around my waist again, and his head tilted toward my shoulder.

"You having fun?" I asked.

He lifted his head so his gorgeous green gaze could lock with mine. "More fun than I would have thought possible two weeks ago at this time."

I grinned and tugged the hat down snugly over Liam's ears. "You look good in my hat."

He chuckled. "Not nearly as good as you look in that sweater."

"This sweater will be burned after next week," I informed him.

Liam only laughed harder. "Sure it will, baby. Keep telling yourself that." He patted my chest and I looked down at his hand on my sweater.

"You know what *really* looks good?" I put my hand over his and rubbed my thumb over the ring on his finger, curving around to the back where Liam had wrapped one of Hazel's hair ribbons around the band multiple times. I'd told him last night that we'd get it sized next week.

"*I'm not taking any chances,*" he'd said.

But honestly? I wasn't worried. The ring was just a ring. It was what it stood for that counted.

"Hey, who's Hazel talking to?" Liam asked, nodding toward the stage where Everett was helping Silas adjust his coat, Parker and Jamie were locked in a Santa-on-Santa embrace that *sounded* way more porn-tastic than it *looked*, and old Jay Turner—the guy whose frail constitution prevented him from leaving the house to notarize our forms—was dancing the Charleston for a bunch of giggling kids.

Off to one side, Hazel stood talking very seriously to a Santa-clad figure who'd bent down on one knee to listen to her. His head was turned away from us, but there was something familiar about his build.

"I don't know," I said. "But I'm almost positive I saw him at the tree lot yesterday."

"They're calling everyone up on stage, right?" Liam said. "We'll find out then."

But by the time all the town Santas—and Jesus Christ,

there were more than *three dozen of them*—had piled on stage to cheers and whistles from the crowd, the Santa I'd been looking for was gone.

Hazel ran over to join us.

"Bug, who was the guy you were talking to?" I searched the faces on the stage.

"Santa."

"I know," I said. "But which? It wasn't Joe Cross, was it?"

She shook her head.

"I know it wasn't Daniel either." I looked to her for confirmation and she shrugged.

"It was *Santa*, Gideon." She rolled her eyes. "And I thanked him *very, very sincerely* for giving me almost everything I asked for because that's *polite*. I got a big house, a cat, and a real Christmas tree. I figure the making-me-a-princess thing might be kinda over his head, so that's fine." She turned back toward the stage, but her eyes met mine over her shoulder. "Oh, and I told him next year would be cool for the whole brother-or-sister thing. I can be patient."

I looked at Liam. Liam looked at me. Both of us turned back toward the stage. Neither of us said a word.

But after Parker had claimed his trophy—because you just *knew* it was gonna be that little nugget of good intentions and outrageous shenanigans who won the freakin' contest, right?—they passed out the Secret Santa presents, and that was when shit really started getting weird.

Hazel got called up to get a brand-new book about the secret lives of cats, and she came back to us beaming. Liam took one of Hazel's hands, and I took the other, and we turned, ready to walk back to town... when Jay Turner called *my* name.

"Gideon Prince Mason," he said, looking down at a

large, flat envelope and then into the crowd, at me, like he'd read it wrong. "*Prince*, Gideon?" He snorted. "Really?"

How*? How*?

How in all the seven layers of *hell* had someone found out my middle name? It wasn't on my driver's license, it wasn't on my social security card, nor my passport, nor my marriage certificate, nor my mortgage, nor any other public record except my *birth certificate*, and legit who in the *world* would go to that trouble?

I stalked toward the stage and took the envelope from Jay with a scowl. "Prince was my mother's maiden name," I said into his microphone. I felt myself blushing. But my embarrassment turned to shock when I actually looked at the address on the envelope.

Liam looked *way* too amused when I returned, until I handed the envelope to him without a word.

"The... The Little Chapel, Las Vegas, Nevada?" His green eyes were wide, and I shook my head because I couldn't explain it either. "The place we were married? Who...?" He glanced up at me in shock.

"Nobody. I've literally told *nobody*, baby."

He ripped open the envelope... and a bunch of pictures fell out. Pictures of a slightly younger me and Liam, in Las Vegas t-shirts. With a short, Russian officiant who looked *nothing* like Elvis.

Someone had given us back our wedding pictures.

"Gideon!" Hazel said excitedly. "If you're a *prince*, does that make Daddy a prince *by marriage?* And if so... does that mean... I'm a *princess?*"

"Yeah, Bug," I agreed hoarsely, picking her up and setting her on my hip. And even though she was way too big for that, she didn't protest. "You're *my* princess, for sure."

Liam, who was sorting through the pictures slack-jawed, held up an unsigned note with one simple word written in bold, black ink: **Believe.**

I ran a hand over my mouth and stared at him.

"Gideon, is it possible—?"

"Nope. No." I shook my head firmly. "It's definitely not."

"But what if—?"

"*No.*"

"But, Gideon—"

I wrapped my arm around him, threading my fingers into the hair at the nape of his neck. "Liam McKnight, you are the love of my life. I have loved you since the moment I met you. I will love you *forever*. And I promise that we will always, *always* talk about the difficult things from now on, okay?"

He nodded.

"But we will never talk about *this* again."

"Never?"

"Not ever."

Liam's lips twitched and his eyes crinkled at the corners. "Okay."

"I mean it."

"No, no, I know." His laughter bubbled over. "Understood."

"I feel like you're *not* understanding, Liam. The laughing thing makes me feel like you're *not* understanding—"

He silenced my protests with a kiss, and Hazel threw her arms around both of us, and for the briefest minute, I felt like I'd somehow gotten stuck in a scene from one of those cheesy TV movies I *never* watched because they were too unrealistic…

Except apparently somehow, unbelievably, this had become my real life.

So, yeah, I would probably never be a nice guy. I'd probably never bother with politeness. And I would *definitely* never have Hazel's ability to believe in Santa —*Christ, no*.

But I was learning that the world really was filled with magic.

Magic was your family and the ridiculous, amazing, generous friends who *became* your family. Magic was the one person in the world who got you and saw something in you that you couldn't see in yourself. Magic was second chances when you least expected them. And magic was *hope*.

Always hope.

Those were things I'd never lose faith in again.

Also by May Archer

The Love in O'Leary Series

The Date (O'Leary #.5)

The Fall (O'Leary #1)

The Gift (O'Leary #2)

The Note (O'Leary 2.5)

The Secret (O'Leary #3)

The World (O'Leary #3.5)

The Fire (O'Leary #4)

The Way Home Series

The Easy Way (The Way Home #1)

The Long Way (The Way Home #2)

The Right Way (The Way Home #3)

M/F Romance Written As Maisy Archer

The Boston Doms Series

About the Author

May lives in Boston. She spends her days raising three incredibly sarcastic children, finding inventive ways to drive her husband crazy, planning beach vacations, avoiding the gym, reading M/M romance, and occasionally writing it. She's also published several M/F romance titles as Maisy Archer.

For free content and the latest info on new releases, sign up for her newsletter at: https://www.subscribepage.com/MayArcher_News

Want to know what projects May has coming up? Check out her Facebook reader group Club May for giveaways, first-look cover reveals, and more.

You can also catch her on Bookbub, and check out her recommended reads!

Made in the USA
Middletown, DE
27 November 2022